I0772952

LOVE'S TRAIL OF REDEMPTION

By Ellen Fannon

BOOK THREE IN THE LOVE IN THE WIND
SERIES

ISBN-13: 978-1-962168-83-0

ALSO BY ELLEN FANNON

Other People's Children
Save the Date – 2022 Christian Indie Award winner
Don't Bite the Doctor
Honor Thy Father – Episode One
Honor Thy Father —Episode Two

LOVE IN THE WIND SERIES
Love in the Wind —Book One —2024 Living Water Award Winner
Falling For a Cowboy – Book Two

Chapter One

"I think tonight's the night!" Olivia Anderson bounced from one foot to the other, which made it difficult to saddle the horse she was preparing for the trail ride at Whispering Winds Ranch where she worked as a guide and riding instructor.

Veterinarian, Darcy Parish, her boss and friend, stopped in mid-tack and stared at her. "Really?" Her face lit up in a huge grin.

Olivia bobbed her head, her honey-blonde ponytail taking on a life of its own with her vigorous movement. "Kyle said he had something important to talk to me about."

Darcy set her saddle on the ground and reached for the cinch strap that, for some reason, Olivia was having trouble fitting through the cinch ring. "You sure are a bundle of nerves." Darcy tightened the strap and turned to face her friend.

Olivia clasped and unclasped her shaking hands in front of her. "I'm sorry. I don't know what's got into me."

"I do. You've got a bad case of the love bug." Darcy finished saddling Olivia's horse while the other woman continued to fidget.

Olivia sighed. "It's just that I've been waiting so long for Kyle to . . . You remember I told you how I had to practically take out a billboard ad to get him to notice me." She rolled her eyes. "And that was two years ago."

Darcy nodded. "Men can be obtuse sometimes. But it sounds like Kyle's finally decided to take the big step." She reached over and gave Olivia a hug. "I'm so happy for you. It's about time."

The sound of a vehicle crunching up the long gravel driveway brought Olivia's mind back into focus. "That will be our riding party. I need to pull myself together." A giggle escaped her lips. "But honestly, I don't know how I'm going to concentrate on this ride. I can't think of anything but tonight. What am I going to wear?"

"Would you like me to take this group? The way you're flitting all over the place, you just might guide them over the side of a cliff." Darcy turned to lead the saddled horse out to the paddock and greet the clients.

Olivia trotted after her. "No, that's okay. I need to keep my mind off Kyle. Only a horse can do that."

Darcy gave her a skeptical look before moving toward the group of people spilling out of the car that had just parked to the side of the stable. "Welcome. I'm Darcy Parish."

Olivia tuned out her employer's introductory speech as she hurried to saddle up the rest of the horses. "Get your mind off Kyle and on your job. Mind off Kyle and . . ." She blew out a frustrated breath. This approach wasn't working. Telling herself to get her mind off Kyle only made the thought of him more acute.

Finally, after two years, he had worked up the courage to pop the question. Olivia had been tempted several times over the past few months to simply ask him to marry her, rather than wait in agony for him to make the move. But deep down, she was old-fashioned and believed the man should propose. She was glad she had waited. Kyle didn't like being pushed, and Olivia knew she tended to be a bit impulsive. What if she had rushed ahead prematurely and scared him off? Although she didn't doubt Kyle's feelings toward her, some men, like Kyle, wanted to do things in their own time.

The anticipation of the coming night caused her heart to dance, and she had to double-check to be sure she had secured the saddle on the next horse properly. The last thing she needed was for a rider to fall off because her head was in the clouds. Her eyes wandered to the two remaining horses standing patiently waiting for her to get them ready and, suddenly, the chore seemed like wading through quicksand. When had she ever experienced inertia when doing the job she loved? A soft whinny from the mare behind her beckoned for her attention. How was she going to get through this trail ride?

Would he already have the ring, or would he ask her to marry him first and then take her ring shopping? It didn't matter. If he gave her a ring, she would love it. Period. As long as she got to spend the rest of her life with Kyle. Her blue dress, that's what she should wear. Even though Kyle had seen it several times, he particularly liked seeing her in it. He always said it brought out the blue in her eyes. Yes, definitely the blue dress. She hoped she had time to wash her hair.

"Olivia? We're ready for you." Darcy's voice carried into the barn where Olivia had stood *not* saddling up horses while her mind had taken off on its own.

She cleared her dry throat. "Uh . . . yes, almost ready." The dust in the barn tickled her nose, and she sneezed several times. No! She couldn't be coming down with a cold. Not now. *Oh, for heaven's sake, Olivia, the musty hay always makes you sneeze. You're not sick. Get a grip on yourself.*

Darcy appeared at the barn door, the sun behind her casting her in a shadow so Olivia could not see the expression on her boss' face. Olivia knew she wasn't hitting on all cylinders today, and after all, despite the fact Darcy was her friend, she still had a business to run. A business that required complete concentration.

"Are you sure you don't want me to fill in?"

Olivia bit her lip. Maybe it would be better if someone led the ride whose head was screwed on tight. Reining in her skittering thoughts right now was like herding cats. "Well, if you really don't mind."

Darcy laughed and moved to the next-to-the-last horse. She placed the pad on its back and hefted the saddle. "Go home, take a warm bath, and make yourself beautiful. And fill me in on all the details tomorrow."

"Okay." Olivia gave in to the rare opportunity to take an early leave. "Thanks, I owe you one."

She walked out of the barn to the looks of an impatient group standing by the paddock. One man pointedly checked his watch.

"I'm sorry," she said, "it will be just a few more minutes." Then, without further explanation, she headed to her car and drove away.

~

Kyle reached across the table and took her hand, as Olivia's heart fluttered against her ribs.

"Have I told you how pretty you look tonight?"

Olivia nodded. "It's okay. You can tell me again." She batted her eyes at him and graced him with her most brilliant smile as she waited for him to go on.

The waiter interrupted the moment as he set their salads before them. Kyle withdrew his hand and picked up his fork.

Olivia's lips pinched in frustration, but she followed his lead. Stabbing a forkful of lettuce and a cherry tomato, she crammed the whole thing into her mouth, stuffing the excess lettuce into her cheeks.

"That's why it's so hard for me to say this."

"Say what?" she mumbled around her mouthful of roughage. Why had she forced so much food into her mouth? Probably because of her nerves. She struggled to chew. Could the man just grow a backbone and ask her already?

Kyle drew in a long breath and jabbed at another bite of salad. Without meeting her eyes, he said, "I think it's time we broke up."

"Wh . . ." Olivia sucked in a breath, pulling the partially chewed lettuce and the cherry tomato into the back of her throat where it lodged firmly. Her gag reflex also got stuck in her throat.

"I mean—" he fiddled with the uneaten greens speared in his fork—"I just don't see our relationship going anywhere, and . . ."

Olivia desperately tried to draw in air and failed. Tears began to leak from the corners of her eyes as she clutched her throat.

"I like you. I like you a lot, but there's just something lacking . . ." His gaze settled on the salad plate in front of him.

Lettuce dribbled from her mouth onto the pristine white tablecloth. Kyle didn't notice because his eyes remained locked on his plate. *A little help here, Kyle?* She tried to make a sound, but nothing came out. It was like one of those dreams where you try to scream, but your voice goes silent. The lack of oxygen was starting to make her panic. How long could a person go without breathing? How long had it already been? What did it matter if she couldn't dislodge this wad of food that blocked her airway and burned her delicate mucous membranes with spicy vinaigrette dressing? How was she going to get Kyle's attention?

Abruptly, she stood, but her oxygen deprivation and hysteria made her weak. Her knees buckled and her hand slammed against the table, rattling silver and dinnerware.

Kyle finally looked up, his brows furrowed in confusion. "Really, Olivia, you don't need to make a scene. I didn't think . . ."

She could feel the fire in her face as she struggled to draw a breath.

"We're two mature adults and . . ."

Desperately, she struggled to remember how to do the Heimlich maneuver on herself, then shoved her mid-section against the edge of the table, making the tableware crash even louder. A couple seated next to them looked over toward the unfolding drama.

"Oh my gosh! She's choking, Howard! Do something!" A disembodied woman's voice floated to Olivia's ears, which buzzed with her racing pulse.

As her vision narrowed into a black tunnel, she felt rough hands reach around her waist and thrust sharply beneath her sternum. The bolus of food shot out of her mouth and hit Kyle's cheek. The cherry tomato bounced off his cheek and rolled across the table, where it finally came to rest against her water glass. Olivia gulped in deep, noisy breaths and collapsed into her chair, tears continuing to stream from her eyes.

"Are you all right, miss?" asked the hero who had saved her life.

She managed to nod. "Thank . . ." Her voice came out in a harsh whisper. The effort to speak brought on a coughing attack, and she fumbled for her napkin.

By now, several onlookers surrounded the table in various stages of confusion and shock.

"What happened?"

"Is she okay?"

"She was choking."

"Good thing someone knew the Heimlich."

"What did she choke on?"

Olivia fought against a wave of nausea. She dipped her napkin in her water glass and pressed it against her forehead. Her eyes flickered open to see Kyle still sitting with dressing dripping down his face, his eyes round and unbelieving.

"I thought she was just upset because I broke up with her," he said, his eyes darting to the group surrounding their table.

The crowd made appropriate comments of disgust.

"Couldn't you see she couldn't breathe?"

"Why didn't you do something?"

"What an idiot."

"Honey, you're better off without him," said a little old lady as she patted Olivia's shoulder. "If you'd been alone with him, the dolt would have let you choke to death."

Olivia continued wiping her face, humiliated and outraged. How dare Kyle dump her? How dare he just sit there while she came within an inch of dying?

"Olivia, I'm sorry. I'm glad you're okay," said Kyle. He still sat like he was bolted to the chair.

She suddenly found her voice. "Sorry? Sorry about what? Almost letting me die, or wasting my time for two years and then breaking up with me?"

"Two years?" echoed a woman to her left. "Girl, I give a guy one year, max. After that, it's adios."

"Yeah, us gals aren't getting any younger."

"Besides, this dude doesn't seem all that bright."

The whole situation suddenly felt hilarious to Olivia, and she began to giggle uncontrollably.

"Come on, sweetie, Howard and I will take you home." Howard's wife put a protective arm around Olivia and drew her from her chair.

Olivia took one final look over her shoulder at the man she thought had been about to ask her to become his wife. The man she'd wanted to spend the rest of her life with. "Wipe your face, Kyle," she said, as she let the older couple lead her away.

Chapter Two

Olivia alternated between sobbing and raging as she poured her heart out to Darcy the next morning.

"Drama, drama, drama," muttered Cam Ellis under his breath as he mucked out the stalls. It wasn't that he lacked sympathy for Olivia—she was a nice kid and all—but he wished they'd move the soap opera out of the barn where he didn't have to overhear the complete play-by-play. Surely they knew he was there. It wasn't as if he was making an effort to be quiet as he went about his work. Did they think simply because he was the hired hand that he was deaf? He wished he'd thought to bring his earbuds and music with him when he'd started on this chore.

Listening to Olivia made him all the more determined not to get involved with a woman. First Ben Parish, his boss, had fallen head-over-heals for Darcy, the pretty veterinarian who had suggested starting trail rides at Whispering Winds Ranch. Then Ricky, the other ranch hand, had taken leave of his good senses with Kendra, a friend of the Parishes. Although the two couples now seemed to be living in blissful wedlock, the drama leading up to the final abandonment of their single days made Cam's stomach twist. Give him the simple, uncomplicated life any day.

Cam pushed a sweaty lock of dark hair from his eyes and reached for his hat. Finally finished with his task, he grasped the handles of the wheelbarrow in his gloved hands and wheeled the pile of manure toward the barn door. The squeaky tire on the wheelbarrow should alert the two women to the fact he was heading their way before he surprised them. He didn't want to intrude on their private conversation. Sometimes, when people became emotionally engaged in a discussion, they forgot others were around and they said things they wished hadn't been overheard.

Ah, just as he thought. As he approached, the ladies suddenly went silent. He nodded his head toward them as he passed, noting that Olivia turned her tear-stained face away from his view. His heart squeezed a little at the raw misery he couldn't avoid seeing, despite Olivia's attempt to hide it. He liked Olivia. They'd worked together for almost two years. Well, not exactly together. He worked for Ben taking care of the Angus cattle at Whispering Winds, as well as the myriad of other duties associated with ranching, while Olivia gave riding lessons and trail rides. Still, their paths crossed frequently enough to be acquainted with her.

She seemed sweet and honest and hard working. And she loved being around the horses. He'd met her boyfriend, Kyle, on a few occasions and, to be honest, had found the guy somewhat immature and self-centered. Of course, he'd kept his opinion to himself, as it wasn't any of his business. But he thought Olivia could do better.

Cam pushed the wheelbarrow out into the yard. The sun made a brief appearance through a curtain in the clouds of the overcast sky, bringing a welcome warmth to the chilly morning. He removed his hat and tipped his head back to the pleasure of the rare moment.

A rough slap on his shoulder jolted him from his brief reprieve. "You working or worshipping the sun?"

Cam shot a sour look at Ricky, who'd come from behind him. Inclining his head to the load in the wheelbarrow, he replied, "How do you think all this manure got here, hmm? I've been at it for an hour. Besides, I didn't see *you* earlier."

"Sorry. The wife made me late." Ricky winked at Cam.

Cam rolled his eyes. "It just goes to prove my point that I'm better off staying single. Too much drama."

Ricky nodded toward the barn. "So, what's up with the cowgirl? She looks mighty upset this morning."

"Her boyfriend broke up with her last night. At least that's what I overheard, not that she told me."

Ricky's lips pressed into a thin line. "Aw, that's too bad." He shook his head. "Poor kid."

Cam shrugged. "Like I said, too much drama." Replacing his hat on his head, he said, "Come on, we've got work to do."

~

Thank goodness for her job. Olivia could always relax when she sat on a horse. Darcy had graciously volunteered to take the first trail riding group this morning, the second time she had taken over Olivia's duties in two days. Olivia could deal with the horses. It was the people she didn't want to be around right now—happy people having fun, couples. How was it that the world around her went on as usual when her shattered heart left her completely disoriented and numb?

Right now, more than anything else, she needed to ride. She saddled up Maggie, her favorite mare, and galloped across the pasture heading to the small brook that ran through the ranch. The feel of the strong, gentle beast beneath her filled her with a sense of control and peace. As though she could outrun her troubles by pushing Maggie to her full speed, Olivia tried to leave the pain behind. The chilly wind against her face and the smell of the newly emerging spring grass both invigorated and calmed her. At first, she didn't notice the tears had started again until she observed the drops falling on the saddle. Wiping a frustrated hand across her eyes, she slowed Maggie as they approached the brook. The mare stopped in the small clearing, her chest heaving from exertion. Olivia slid from the saddle and patted the animal's neck. She knew Maggie enjoyed going at full throttle.

"Thank you, dear girl. You're the best friend anyone could ever have." Olivia rested her forehead against the sweaty mare and breathed in the earthy scent of horse that, to her, was more aromatic than the finest perfume. "You deserve a break." She released the reins so Maggie could graze while Olivia stepped toward the brook.

She found a flat, sun-warmed rock and sank onto it, drawing her knees up to her chest while the burbling flow of water over stones mesmerized her with its sweet melody. Allowing the soothing sound to comfort her hurting heart, Olivia filled her lungs with the clear, fresh air.

"What now, God?" she whispered. "I thought Kyle was the one." After two years, she thought she'd known the man. It was sobering and disturbing how little she apparently had known. Had she been blinded by her love for him? Had she missed obvious red flags? She searched her mind objectively to analyze what had gone wrong but came up blank. When and where had their relationship taken on two such different courses? Her course had led toward wanting a lifetime commitment, and his had led toward discontentment and wanting his freedom. As far as she knew, everything was fine—better than fine. Her head snapped up. Was there another woman? Frowning, she racked her brain again, searching for signs. Kyle had always seemed loyal, never giving her a moment of doubt, never flirting with another woman in her presence, never talking excessively about another woman.

A deep sigh flowed through her lips. It didn't really matter how or where or when Kyle had become tired of the relationship. He had made it clear last night that he wanted out, and although her heart felt as though he had trampled on it, she didn't want to be with someone who didn't want to be with her. She deserved better. Her thoughts replayed the terrifying choking episode of the previous evening and how Kyle had been totally clueless. Had he always been so oblivious to events around him? Had he always been so selfish?

She remembered the first time she'd seen Kyle on the campus in Jackson when she had been running an errand for her previous employer at the agricultural center, and her heart had flip-flopped like a dying fish inside her chest. Tall and muscular, with wavy blond hair and twinkling blue eyes, he had held the door open for her as she entered the building, then, to her surprise, he had been waiting outside when she finished. He was an animal science major, and they hit it off immediately. Still, it had taken a while before they officially became a couple, and she ruminated on the way she'd had to push a little to make that happen. At the time, she'd attributed his reticence to shyness, but in retrospect, perhaps he hadn't been all that keen about taking their relationship to a more serious level even back then. Had she missed that sign? He'd seemed content enough. She thought they were more than compatible, with her working with horses and him hoping to get into veterinary school. But maybe their interest in animals was all they had in common.

As she mused, she remembered that Kyle hadn't been particularly eager to socialize with her circle of friends, something she found strange since Darcy, as a veterinarian, could have been a great mentor to him. His faith, although he claimed to be a Christian, also seemed weak. Church wasn't a priority for him like it was for her, but she'd hoped he'd change once they were married, especially when they had children. Yes, she'd definitely overlooked *that* aspect of his character. Still, many men had become stronger Christians as a result of their believing wives.

A soft snort from Maggie broke into her thoughts, and Olivia realized it was time to go. She couldn't sit here brooding all day. She still had a job to do, and she couldn't expect Darcy to cover for her indefinitely. But the future seemed uncertain and bleak. Pushing to her feet, she walked the short distance back to where she'd left Maggie grazing and climbed up into the saddle. This time, she walked the mare slowly back to the stable, not in any hurry to return to her now empty life.

Chapter Three

"Now that Olivia is free, why don't you ask her to go with you to Bill and Audrey's wedding next week?" Ricky nudged Cam with his elbow as they finished making the rounds of the ranch and dismounted from their horses.

Cam stopped in his tracks and gaped at Ricky. "Are you crazy? Why would you even suggest such a thing?"

Ricky shrugged as he led his horse, Windsong, to the barn. "Your invitation says 'plus one' and she probably doesn't want to go by herself now that her 'plus one' is no longer around."

Cam hissed an exasperated breath through his lips. "In the first place," he said, as he undid the noseband and throat latch on Malachi, "I probably won't even go to the wedding. I don't know them all that well."

"They hang out here all the time with the rest of the church group. You know them well enough to get an invite to their wedding." Ricky removed the saddle from Windsong and set it on the ground.

"Yeah, well, they were probably just being polite.

I don't even go to church with the rest of your crowd."

Ricky raised his eyebrows at Cam's reference to "your crowd."

"What? Since you and Kendra got together, you're all one big happy church family. I don't fit in with the rest of the group." Cam hadn't meant to speak those last few words aloud, but the fact was he had felt a bit of disconnect when Ricky had joined the church where Ben and Darcy and the rest of their friends attended. Although he was probably being oversensitive, Cam suddenly felt more like a mere employee than a friend. It hadn't been so bad when he and Ricky were both just ranch hands, but now Ricky was part of the inner circle, and Cam felt as though he were on the outside looking in.

To make matters even more complicated, Ricky had dropped a bombshell on them all a few months previously by admitting he had a Ph.D. in physics. Cam couldn't quite wrap his head around the fact that Ricky preferred being a cowboy to making good money as a scientist. But Ricky had recently started teaching physics part-time at the STEM school where his wife, Kendra, taught biology. When Cam wanted to push Ricky's buttons, he called him "professor." Generally, the change in their status didn't bother him until something like Bill and Audrey's wedding came up.

"Come on, man, nobody treats you any differently. What's second?"

"What?" Cam scrunched his brows.

"You said, 'In the first place.' What's second?" Ricky patted Windsong's rump as she headed into her stall. Then he crossed his arms along the fence rail and leveled a piercing gaze at Cam.

Cam shook his head, trying to reorient his thoughts. What had they been talking about? Oh, yeah. Taking Olivia to the wedding. "Second, I'm not interested in taking a date. And third, even if I were interested, I'm much too old for Olivia."

Ricky picked up his saddle and headed to the tack room. Cam closed the gate on Malachi's stall and followed. Even though this conversation was absurd, and he had no wish to continue it, he still had to clean and put away the tack.

"How old do you think Olivia is?" Ricky asked, reaching for a rag hanging on a hook.

Irritation rose in Cam's chest. "I don't know. Twenty? Twenty-one?" He slammed his saddle onto the saddle rack a little harder than he'd intended.

"She's twenty-five."

"And I'm thirty-two. I'm practically old enough to be her—"

"Big brother." Ricky shot him an annoying grin.

Cam clenched his jaw. "Look, don't start on me. I'm a happily confirmed bachelor."

Ricky hung up the rest of his tack. "I didn't ask you to marry her. I only suggested it might be nice for her not to have to attend the wedding alone."

Cam didn't reply. He finished putting away his gear in silence, his back turned to Ricky to avoid encouraging any more conversation.

~

"Would you like Ben and me to pick you up for the wedding tomorrow?" Darcy asked.

Olivia groaned. She'd just managed to finish her last riding lesson with her body and mind on autopilot and was making her escape to her car to head home and soak in a hot tub. Maybe she'd never get out. These last few days had been pure torture. It seemed that everywhere she looked there were happy couples. She couldn't ever remember being envious of someone else's good fortune, but now her heart seized every time Ben put his arm around Darcy or couples teased each other on the trail rides. Kendra had even shown up last night for no good reason other than to flaunt her happily married status in Olivia's face. Okay, that last thought wasn't fair. Kendra had always been kind to her, and she'd been sympathetic to the news of Olivia's and Kyle's breakup. It was just that Ricky acted like such a . . . a devoted puppy whenever his new bride was around. Ricky, of all people. The tough, taciturn cattle wrangler had let a woman wrap him around her little finger.

And the last thing Olivia wanted to do this weekend was attend a wedding. She couldn't bear watching another couple make a lifelong commitment to each other to live together in marital bliss. Especially when she thought she'd be making her own wedding plans. She wished she'd managed to leave before Darcy caught up with her at the car.

Olivia chewed on her lip. "Um, I don't think I'll go. I'm really not feeling up to it."

Darcy's eyes shone with concern, and she took a step forward.

Olivia took a step back and turned to her car. *Don't hug me now or I'll burst into tears.* She knew Darcy was only trying to help, but there was nothing she could do, and Olivia couldn't stand the pity she saw in her friend's eyes.

"Sweetie, I know you're hurting right now."

Darcy's soft voice reached Olivia's ear through the whooshing of the gentle wind that had picked up as the sun had begun its rapid descent in the dusky sky.

Whispering Winds. What a perfect name for this place. A momentary peace calmed her heart as though God, Himself, had touched her with a soft caress. Then she felt a more tangible caress as Darcy reached out and brushed her shoulder. She still couldn't turn around and face Darcy lest she start crying and never be able to stop.

Darcy spoke to her back. "But I think it would do you good to get out and be around people instead of sitting home by yourself."

Maybe. But not a wedding, of all things.

"Look, I'll call you tomorrow. If you still don't feel like going, we won't push you." Darcy gave Olivia's shoulder a little squeeze.

Olivia could only nod. Then she slid into her car and, without looking at her friend, headed down the long driveway to her apartment, feeling lonelier than she could ever remember having felt before.

Chapter Four

Saturday morning, a veil of sadness descended on Olivia the moment she opened her eyes. As she struggled out of her sleep-induced fog, the feeling only intensified. Why should she be so blue today? Then she remembered. Not only was this the day of *the wedding*, but she didn't have to work. The whole day stretched ahead of her with nothing to fill the empty hours. Her apartment didn't need to be cleaned. Over the past few evenings, she had already scrubbed her small living area spotless in an effort to take her mind off her situation and diffuse nervous energy. Hard manual labor helped keep her from brooding.

So, what should she do today? Ordinarily, she would have gone out to the ranch and hung out. But she didn't want to be around people. She could take a long ride on one of the horses, but she would still have to interact with everyone at the ranch, and she didn't want to be nagged into attending the wedding that she had no intention of going to. Maybe she should take a few hours and go shopping. She hadn't been to the grocery store in a couple of weeks and probably needed a few items. She hadn't really paid much attention to her supplies since she hadn't eaten much these past few days. Yet the idea of pushing a buggy through a crowd full of strangers seemed less than appealing. Besides, she doubted she had the energy to get out of bed, let alone go out in public.

She picked up her phone from her bedside table and scrolled through her social media, becoming more depressed as she read about all her friends' exciting adventures and viewed their happy pictures. Was she the only one in the world who was miserable? Not that she wanted other people to be miserable, she just wanted to be happy again.

The thought that Kyle dumping her could have such a profound impact on her state of mind filled her gut with fiery anger. How could one man have that much power over her? Was Kyle wallowing in self-pity right now? Was he missing her and regretting his decision? Was he miserable without her? It seemed unlikely, as he'd not contacted her since the breakup. Not even to be sure she was okay after nearly choking to death. Well, to heck with him. If he could discard her so easily, he wasn't worth space in her head or her heart. It was time she took back her life and made her own happiness—happiness that didn't include Kyle.

"Out, Kyle," she said. "I don't need you to complete me. I'm just fine all by myself." She threw off the covers and hopped out of bed.

Replacing the hurt with anger helped motivate her into the shower and, as she stood under the hot spray, her mind explored all the positive opportunities she could consider now that she had more time on her hands. The problem was she couldn't readily think of any new hobbies or activities at the moment. No worries, something great would turn up. She just had to trust God to lead her in a different direction.

She realized since the breakup she had indirectly blamed God for the fact things had not turned out the way she'd wanted. A saying she had heard somewhere popped into her brain. "God never wastes a hurt." If she believed, as she claimed to believe, that God was in control, she would have to trust He had her back. Losing Kyle wasn't the worst thing that had ever happened to her. Marrying a man who didn't share her feelings would have been far worse.

Olivia turned off the shower and wrapped herself in a thick towel. Wiping the steam from the mirror, she critically examined her reflection. She'd allowed her sadness to rob her eyes of their sparkle and create dark circles under them. No more! Starting today she would end the grieving over Kyle and look for new ways to fulfill her life—including attending Bill and Audrey's wedding. A prick of pain jabbed her heart at the thought of the wedding, but she refused to allow it to continue poking at her.

"I will go to that wedding and I will sincerely wish the bride and groom a wonderful life together, and I *will* have a good time. Even if it kills me," she said to the woman in the mirror who stared back with renewed resolve in her eyes and an upward tilt of her chin.

~

Several hours later, Olivia sat alone watching other couples dancing, and her resolve crumbled. Frustrated by her appearance that morning, she'd taken extra care to make herself look pretty. Ordinarily, with her job, hair and makeup were not a high priority. Nor were her clothes. But for tonight, Olivia wanted to look feminine. She had taken a curling iron to her straight blonde hair—which she usually wore pulled back in a ponytail—forming soft waves that framed her oval face. Carefully applied makeup concealed the dark rings under her eyes, which she'd enhanced with eyeliner and mascara. A few strokes of soft pink blush gave her pale cheeks a healthy glow. Her short, coral, handkerchief hem dress and high-heeled silver sandals showed off her shapely legs. She'd bought the dress on a whim and stuck it in her closet where it remained forgotten and never worn. Perusing her limited collection of suitable dressy clothes, she had happened upon the overlooked garment and decided it would be perfect for a wedding.

Not being part of the bridal party, she had been seated at a table of people she didn't know, which only added to her sense of feeling alone and left out. The seat next to her, which should have been occupied by Kyle, remained conspicuously vacant. The other couples around the table, after a few minutes of polite chit-chat with her, had naturally fallen back to conversing among themselves before they got up to dance, leaving her sitting by herself. Ben, Darcy, Ricky, and Kendra would occupy seats at the head table when and if the wedding photographer ever finished with pictures. Olivia wished they'd return so she'd have someone to talk to. In retrospect, coming to this wedding had not only failed to lift her spirits, it had plunged her deeper into her self-pity. Well, she was not going to sit here like an overlooked wallflower. Even if she didn't know anyone, she would force herself to mingle.

Pushing herself out of her chair, her ankle twisted as she stood on the high heels she was unaccustomed to wearing. Served her right for trying to be "girly," something she wasn't. Give her old blue jeans and boots, and she could handle anything. Almost. But dressed like a supermodel? Who was she trying to kid? Who was she trying to impress? She should have stuck to simple and basic. Okay, mingling might be a little too ambitious, given the leaden feeling in her stomach, but maybe she could at least get a bottle of water from the bar. She took a tentative step, acclimating to the impractical, but flashy footwear. Blast these stupid shoes. After wobbling halfway across the room, her ankle turned again, and she reached out to steady herself against a chair occupied by a plump, matronly woman who shot her a disapproving stare at being jostled.

"Sorry," she muttered as the older lady pursed her lips.

Why did I come here? Her spirits plummeted lower with each unsteady step.

Chapter Five

Cam leaned against the wall and surveyed the room with a bored eye. Why had he let his friends talk him into coming to this wedding? The only people he knew were tied up doing wedding pictures and, at this rate, the reception would probably be over before they showed up. He made up his mind to wait until the wedding party made an appearance, then he would wish them well and escape. The old movie channel had a western scheduled for eight o'clock tonight, which sounded infinitely more appealing than hanging around this reception.

A woman who appeared to be either inebriated or walking on eggshells caught his eye. He watched in amusement as she tottered to the bar, her swingy dress falling gracefully over well-shaped legs, despite her less-than-graceful gait. Silky blonde hair hung just past her shoulders, but her face was turned away from him. Curiosity got the better of him as he waited to see if she would order an alcoholic beverage. Then he remembered that Bill and Audrey had emphatically vetoed alcohol at their wedding. Too many horror stories of intoxicated guests causing scenes and ruining the event reinforced their decision. So, if the woman was drunk, she would've had to imbibe before the ceremony, which seemed unlikely. As he continued to observe the odd lady, he saw the bartender hand her a bottle of water. His eyes followed her as she tottered back to her seat at an empty table as fast as she could manage in her spiky shoes. Only when she settled into her chair and tipped the bottle back to take a long drink did recognition dawn.

Olivia? Surely that beautiful woman couldn't be Olivia. Well, why couldn't it be her? He knew she'd been invited to the wedding, as Ricky had so unsubtly pointed out. Cam had merely been surprised at her appearance, that's all. He couldn't remember ever having seen her wearing anything but jeans and T-shirts or sweatshirts. Or wearing her hair down, for that matter. He studied her from his vantage point. The kid cleaned up rather well. *Very* well, in fact. He supposed he should really stop thinking of her as a kid, although she looked like she was fresh out of high school. If Ricky was right about her age, she was much older than Cam had thought. Still too young for him—not that he was looking—but a woman, nevertheless, not a kid. He watched her sag into the chair as though the weight of the world pressed down on her, then remembered her boyfriend had dumped her. Duh. That explained why she sat by herself and looked like she wanted to disappear.

Cam supposed he should be polite and at least say hello. Neither one of them appeared to be having a good time, and they did work together, after all. He pushed himself off the wall and sauntered across the room to hover over her. She seemed miles away, lost in her thoughts.

"Hey," he said.

She jumped and looked up. "Cam? Oh, hi. I didn't know you were coming."

He snorted. "Yeah, I got invited. Not sure why, but here I am. I didn't want to be rude. Not that the wedding party would notice, since they've yet to show up."

A sad smile touched the corners of her mouth. "Yeah, I kind of felt like I should come to be polite, but I'm getting tired of waiting for the wedding party, too. When I get married, I'm not going to hold the guests hostage while we take wedding pictures. We'll do them before the ceremony. I don't care about tradition." Then her face crumpled as she apparently realized what she'd said.

He ignored her last comment, as no wedding loomed in her future, and he didn't want to let on that he knew and make her feel worse. Should he sit with her? She hadn't invited him to join her, but she sure looked like she could use some company. "May I?" He tipped his head to the empty seat next to her.

Her gaze followed his to the unoccupied chair. "Oh. Yeah, sure." She didn't offer any explanation of why her plus-one seat was vacant. Surely she knew the word on her new single status had gotten around, even if she hadn't been aware that he'd heard every word she'd poured out to Darcy in the barn the other day.

Cam pulled out the chair and dropped into it. Uncomfortable silence stretched between them while their eyes surveyed everything in the room but each other. Finally, he said, "You look nice tonight."

She turned and peered directly at him, a quirky

smile dancing about her lips. "As opposed to how I usually look?"

He chuckled. "I didn't mean it that way. I've just never seen you all dressed up."

She sighed. "Yeah, well, I'm way out of my comfort zone." Her eyes traveled over him. "You look nice, too, by the way. I'm not sure I've ever seen you in a suit and tie."

Cam tugged at his neck. "Talk about being out of your comfort zone. This tie is about to strangle me."

"Why don't you take it off?"

He mulled the idea over. Why not? "You know something? I just might do that." He reached up and undid the knot, releasing the irksome strip of cloth and laying it on the table in front of him. Then he opened his top shirt button. "Ah, that's better. I can breathe again."

She laughed. "I suppose once a cowboy, always a cowboy."

"You got that right."

Her eyes drifted back to the couples on the dance floor. Did she want to dance? Should he ask her? It seemed like the right thing to do, but would it be weird? They really didn't know each other all that well. Still, it was just dancing, it wasn't like it meant anything. His throat suddenly felt tight, despite loosening his shirt and tie, but as he continued to follow her line of sight, he felt obligated to ask.

"Would you like to dance?"

She turned back to him, hesitancy in her eyes. Then she dropped her gaze and swallowed. "Um, I'm really not very good. Plus, I can barely walk in these shoes, let alone dance." She stuck her feet out, displaying the stunning, but impractical footwear.

"Kick 'em off."

Her eyebrows raised. "What? Seriously?"

"Sure, why not? If I can shed my tie, you can shed your shoes."

She chewed on her lip for a second, then nodded. "Okay." She bent and unbuckled the straps around her ankles, wiggling her feet free. A blush crept into her cheeks when she caught him staring at her.

He stood and held out his hand. "Shall we?"

As she slid her hand into his, Cam realized he had never touched her before. What a silly thought. Why would he have touched her, other than on the occasions when they happened to brush against each other when working with a horse? A fleeting thought crossed his mind of how natural her hand felt in his. She had soft hands, yet, at the same time, they were strong. He'd seen how she handled horses with quiet strength and confidence. He had always admired her natural ability with the animals, as well as being able to pull her own weight on the ranch.

They found a space on the periphery of the dance floor, and he rested his other hand gently against her back, taking in the silkiness of her hair as it spilled over his hand. With a large gap between their bodies, they shuffled to the music with somewhat clumsy movements. Even with the space separating them, Cam became aware that she smelled sweet, whether from a flowery soap, shampoo, or perfume, he couldn't tell. He'd never noticed a scent on her body before, not that he'd been checking. If anything, she usually smelled like horses. He bent his head closer to hers. The fragrance came from her shampoo. He rested his cheek against her head, breathing in the pleasant aroma. Who would have thought little tomboy Olivia could be so feminine? At least that's how he'd always thought of her. Sort of like his pesky younger sister, Annette, who'd always trailed after him wanting to be one of the boys.

He tried to push the thought of Annette from his mind. Their strained relationship over the past few years had yet to improve, despite his wishing otherwise. Once so close, she had held him at arm's length since the "incident," as he had come to think of it, and no amount of apologizing or trying to make up for what had happened could move her. Granted, he took full blame and responsibility, but at some point, he just wanted his little sister back. Couldn't she cut him some slack and forgive him?

A sigh escaped his lips, and Olivia looked up at him, her eyes questioning. "Something wrong? Did I step on your feet?"

He forced a smile. "No, my mind was wandering. Sorry." Then he realized how insensitive that sounded when his mind should have been on dancing with her.

"I understand," she said, and as he studied her face, he figured her mind was probably wandering, too. She was probably wishing she was in the arms of her long-time boyfriend instead of a casual work acquaintance.

Just then, the bridal party finally made their appearance, and the couples on the dance floor broke apart to applaud and congratulate them. Ricky, with Kendra on his arm, came up and clapped Cam on the back, his eyes darting between him and Olivia. Ricky gave him a knowing wink. Cam's lips tightened, but he wouldn't say anything in front of Olivia.

"You look great for a cowgirl," Ricky said to her.

"What a beautiful dress," Kendra chimed in.

"Thank you," Olivia murmured. Then, as if realizing she should return the compliment, she added, "It was a lovely ceremony. I love the bridesmaids' dresses."

Kendra laughed. "Thank goodness Audrey has good taste. You wouldn't believe some of the bridesmaids' dresses I've worn. I think the bride deliberately picked them to make us look awful so she could look beautiful by comparison."

"They're motioning for us to be seated," said Ricky. "See you two later."

Standing awkwardly on the dance floor, Cam almost wished he'd ducked out before the bridal party came in. Now they would have to sit through the toasts and all the other hoopla that went along with a big wedding. He supposed he should escort Olivia back to the table, but should he sit with her? He glanced at her table and noticed the other couples had taken their places.

Olivia headed toward her table, then turned and looked at him over her shoulder. He trailed after her, then remained standing as she settled into her chair. A couple of the men stood and extended their hands, introducing themselves, so he did the same.

"Are you Olivia's boyfriend?" asked one of the women.

Olivia's face reddened to a deep crimson, and Cam's words got caught in his throat. "Uh, no, we're . . ." *We're what?* "Friends" sounded so impersonal, and didn't seem to quite define their status.

"We work together," Olivia interjected.

The talk turned briefly to where they worked before Ben tapped his water glass to get everyone's attention.

Cam tuned out the toasts, which went on way too long, and from the glazed look in Olivia's eyes, she did too. At one point, he leaned in and whispered, "I don't know about you, but I'm not a big fan of these drawn-out wedding receptions."

She nodded and shot him a knowing smile. "But it seems we're trapped for the time being."

"So, let's kill the time until we can politely make an exit."

She angled her body toward him. "Okay, what do you suggest?" A teasing flicker of light danced in her eyes.

"Why don't you tell me about some of your trail-riding clients? I know you have some great stories, especially about the city slickers."

A huge grin stretched across her face as a laugh bubbled from her lips. It felt nice to hear her laugh after so many days of her walking around wrapped in a cloud of gloom. "Cam, that's not nice. By the way, what does 'Cam' stand for?"

Her question caught him off-guard. "Nothing. Just 'Cam.' Why?"

"Oh, I thought it might be short for Cameron or Camden or something."

"Okay, now that we've cleared that mystery up, back to your stories."

She wagged a finger at him. "Maybe another time. I hope they cut the cake soon so we can get out of here." Then, seeming to realize she'd said, "we," she stammered, "I mean, I'm tired and want to get out of these clothes."

He pictured her back in her customary attire, and the thought occurred to him that he would never quite look at her the same way again. "We don't have to wait. How about we sneak out? That is unless you really have a craving for cake."

She pressed her lips together, considering, then nodded. "I guess that's one advantage to being seated in the back. No one will notice if we leave."

Cam grinned. "Come on." He snatched his tie from the table and automatically reached for her hand. She scooped her shoes from the floor, and they hurried from the reception hall out to the foyer.

Olivia giggled as they sped toward the door. "I have this feeling we're doing something naughty and I should feel more guilty."

"The guilt factor only adds to the fun." He held the door open for her, and she preceded him into the parking lot, her shoes dangling from her hand. "Where's your car?"

She let go of his hand and pointed down the row of vehicles in the rear next to a row of box hedges.

"I'll walk you to your car."

"You don't have to. I'm perfectly fine."

"I want to. A gentleman doesn't leave a lady stranded in a dark parking lot."

She snorted.

"What's so funny?"

The edges of her lips tipped into a smile. "You. Being all chivalrous. I've never considered myself a 'lady.' Besides, you've never even offered to carry a saddle for me."

His eyebrows rose. "I never knew you wanted me to."

"I didn't. It's just . . . oh never mind. This whole evening has been so . . ." She let her words trail off as she laid a hand on his arm. "Thank you for rescuing me from a potentially miserable night."

His eyebrows rose. "Rescuing?"

She rolled her eyes. "Poor choice of words. You know what I mean. I actually enjoyed myself toward the end."

"My pleasure. I wasn't exactly having the time of my life, either." They walked to where her Camri sat dwarfed by two pickup trucks.

She fumbled in her purse for her keys and opened the door, then lingered a moment, regarding his face as if seeing it for the first time.

"Seriously, thanks again."

"You're welcome. Anytime." He held the door as she slid inside, then leaned in. "Well, to be honest, I hope there won't be another time like this, but if there is, we can be each other's plus-one."

She grinned. "It's a deal."

"Oh, and tell me which horse you want saddled on Monday, and I'll have it ready for you."

Olivia laughed. "I think I can handle it."

He shut her car door and waited as she pulled out of the parking lot, waving as she exited. Well, the evening hadn't been a complete waste. It had actually turned out kind of nice. Getting to know Olivia a little better had been an unexpected bonus.

Chapter Six

The evening replayed through Olivia's mind like a movie with an unexpected twist at the end. Just when she'd felt as though she'd made a huge mistake by going to the wedding, and was feeling her most vulnerable and exposed, Cam had shown up. She winced when she remembered telling him he had rescued her, but truthfully, she had enjoyed their brief time together.

A red flag popped up front and center of her wandering thoughts. *Cam is not a rebound. He's a nice guy you work with who just hung out with you because you were both alone.* Or, worse yet, he felt sorry for her. Mortification swept through her gut at the thought he may have kept her company out of pity. Was that the reason he came over to her table? Thankfully, he hadn't brought up the absence of Kyle, although he had to know about the breakup. She hadn't exactly been quiet when she'd bared her broken heart to Darcy. She had been aware of Cam's presence in the barn, although, at the time, she'd been in too much pain to care who overheard. Now she wished she'd been a little more discreet.

She hoped things wouldn't be weird between them when she saw him at the ranch on Monday. But then, why should they be? She had no intention of targeting him for "new boyfriend material." Then her memory conjured up her comment about how photographs would be done at *her* wedding, and she felt her face flushing even though she was by herself. How many other stupid comments had she made? Did Cam think she was flirting or trying to pursue him? Gracious, she hoped not! That would be the last thing she needed, a man who feared she'd set her sights on him. She would just have to be careful not to appear to come on too strong. Great. Now work *would* be weird. Where was the line between friendly and man-hungry?

You're reading way more into this evening than was there. Let it go. But her warm feeling had suddenly turned clammy.

~

"Maggie's all saddled up and ready for you." Cam stood by the paddock, a goofy grin on his face as Olivia headed to the barn on Monday morning.

Olivia's cheeks stretched into a wide smile at the sight of the beautiful mare standing ready to go for the first trail ride of the day. "How did you know I wanted Maggie?"

Cam shrugged. "I know she's your favorite. I figured you'd want her."

A flood of warmth surged through her body at the fact Cam knew she favored Maggie. He was apparently more observant than she had given him credit for. "I didn't realize you knew she was my favorite."

"It's not hard to figure out. You almost always ride her."

"True. I guess it's fairly obvious. I just didn't think you would have particularly noticed."

He chuckled. "I'm not quite as dumb as I look."

She laughed with him. "I'm not sure how to respond to your last statement. So, do you want to saddle up the other four horses I need for this morning?"

He reached for his hat hanging on the gate post and settled it on his head. "Nope, that's my one good deed for the day. I've got work to do." He unlatched the gate and headed to another horse he'd readied to make his rounds of the ranch.

Her tone turned serious. "Cam, thank you. For everything."

"Any time," he replied as he mounted Giovani and headed back through the open gate. "By the way, you look more like your old self today."

"Thank you, I think."

"I meant it as a compliment. A horsewoman naturally becomes you." He tipped his hand to his hat and trotted off.

"Have a good day," she called after him, realizing she felt better than she had for the past several days.

"Did you have a good time at the wedding?"

Darcy's unexpected appearance startled her as she stood gazing after Cam. Turning, she saw her boss and friend walking toward the paddock wearing her baggy coveralls and boots, ready to head out to work.

Olivia hesitated. "Yes and no."

"I understand. I'm sorry we couldn't sit with you. And the pictures took forever." Darcy blew out an exasperated breath, then brightened. "But I saw you and Cam dancing. Did you two hang out together?"

"Only for a little while." Olivia lowered her eyes, not wanting Darcy to get the wrong impression. "He was nice enough to come over and talk to me when he saw me sitting alone."

Darcy laid a hand on Olivia's arm. "Cam's a good man."

Olivia didn't know why, but Darcy's comment irritated her. "I'm not looking for a man, good or otherwise." Her words came out snippier than she'd intended and, glancing up, she noted the hurt in Darcy's eyes.

Darcy removed her hand. "Honestly, Olivia, I didn't mean to imply anything. I know you're still hurting over Kyle."

"I'm fine about Kyle. But I'm not looking to jump into another relationship. I need some time to myself." Surely Darcy had to understand, having been through a similar situation after her fiancé had dumped her. She'd even moved to Wyoming to start a new life.

"I know you do. And I'm here for you, you know that."

Darcy stepped forward as if to give her a hug, but Olivia stiffened and backed away. She didn't want to dissect her feelings right now, and her emotions were still raw. "I need to get ready for the first group of riders."

Darcy nodded. "And I need to get to work. See you later."

Chapter Seven

"Are you sure you'll be okay while Ben and I are away?" Darcy asked for the hundredth time. She and Ben were flying to Pennsylvania to visit Darcy's parents for a few days before things got busier toward the summer.

"For the last time, we'll be fine," Olivia replied. "I'll just be doing the trail rides and riding lessons, as usual. Cam and Ricky are the ones with the hard job of overseeing the ranch."

Darcy gazed at her for a moment too long, and Olivia knew Darcy was still worried about her emotional stability since the breakup. But it had been three weeks, and Olivia had given her no cause for concern. Other than the day after Kyle dumped her, she'd done her job competently and cheerfully. Okay, maybe not exactly cheerfully. But she thought she'd faked her way through fairly convincingly. She'd become good at compartmentalizing her feelings and keeping from wearing her aching heart on her sleeve. If only she didn't feel so empty inside. It wasn't that she wanted Kyle back, but the thought of being alone again after being used to having someone in her life filled her with the sense of being adrift with no anchor.

Olivia forced a smile."You go and have a wonderful time, and don't worry about this place," Olivia added, giving her friend a playful shove toward the truck where Ben waited to drive them to the airport. Besides, what would Darcy do if Olivia said she wouldn't be okay? Cancel the trip? It had merely been a rhetorical question.

~

Six hours later, Olivia's stress level skyrocketed as she finished her last lesson and found Dandy rolling in his stall. He hadn't been acting himself earlier on the trail ride, and she had substituted another horse for the next group. Now he was down and rolling, a sure sign of colic. She should have noticed that he hadn't touched his food and he pawed the ground when she put him back in his stall, but she'd been in a hurry to get to the next group of people who were waiting. How long had he been down? Why hadn't she alerted Cam or Ricky? Well, because she hadn't seen either of them all day and, if she were truthful, she had kind of forgotten. Her words to Darcy came back to haunt her.

We'll be fine. Now one of the horses was sick and her negligence may have made the situation worse. Colic was a potentially life-threatening condition. And, of course, Dandy had to colic within a few hours after his veterinarian owner left town. She needed to get help fast.

Olivia grabbed a lead rope and attached it to the animal's halter. "Come on, boy, up." She yanked on the halter, trying to encourage the horse to stand. Allowing him to roll could result in injury.

Dandy tossed his head, resisting at first, then managed to get his legs under him.

"Let's get you out to the paddock where you can walk." She led him toward the open barn door and outside to the fenced-in area where she taught riding lessons. Sometimes walking a colicky horse helped with the abdominal pain and helped increase gut motility.

As she got him into the open area, she pressed a hand to the angle behind his jaw to feel for his pulse. Consulting her watch, she counted fifty beats per minute. His pulse rate was a little high, but he had been rolling, so it wasn't overly alarming. Next, she lifted his lip and checked his gum color, which was slightly red, but not terribly abnormal. But the dryness of his gums concerned her. She pressed her finger against the gum to blanch the tissue and, again, consulted her watch to monitor the capillary refill time, or how long it took for the color to return to the gums. Two seconds. Okay, good. Longer than three seconds could indicate shock or dehydration. She watched his chest movements, registering his respiratory rate, which was also a little elevated, but probably not excessive considering he had been rolling for a period of time, the length of which she didn't know. Last, she stepped to his side and, pulling her hair away from her face, put her ear next to his flank to listen for gut sounds. His clammy skin against her cheek initially startled her until she reminded herself the animal would be sweating after rolling.

"What on earth are you doing?" came an amused male voice.

Olivia straightened to see Cam leading Malachi back to the barn after the afternoon check of the cattle. Relief surged through her at his appearance. She hadn't even realized how scared she'd been until she suddenly found she wasn't alone.

"Dandy was rolling in his stall. We need to call a vet."

Worry lines replaced Cam's smile as he moved toward the distressed animal. Releasing Malachi into the paddock, he stepped closer and laid a hand behind Dandy's jaw.

"His pulse is fifty, respirations twenty-two, capillary refill time two seconds, gums are slightly tacky, and gum color mildly reddened. I was checking for gut sounds."

Cam's smile returned. "Good job. I should have known you'd have everything under control. Has he passed any stool?"

Olivia shook her head. "Not since I moved him out here. I didn't check his stall. But I did notice he hadn't eaten."

"I'll examine his stall and call the vet. Why does Darcy have to be gone today of all days?"

"This is the first colic I've seen since I've been working here," Olivia said.

"Fortunately, it hasn't happened frequently," Cam said, as he pulled his cell phone from his pocket and walked toward the barn. "I hope Dr. Lockhart is on call. I like him better than the other guy Darcy works with."

Olivia watched Cam disappear into the barn and heard his muffled one-sided conversation with someone from Darcy's clinic. She reached up a hand to calm the painful animal who swished his tail and kept looking at his flank. Having been interrupted from listening for gut sounds, she moved back to his midsection and, once again, stuck her ear to his side, noting he wasn't sweating as profusely as he had been a few minutes earlier. But the silence of normal burbling coming from his abdomen was cause for concern.

Cam returned to the paddock, his confident steps comforting her unease. He tucked his phone back into his pocket and said, "No stool. Dr. Lockhart is on his way. It shouldn't be too long. In the meantime, he said to check Darcy's box for flunixin and give Dandy 10 cc's."

"I'll look. I know where she keeps it." Olivia handed the lead rope to him and headed to the house. She unlocked the kitchen door and flipped on the overhead lights, bathing the rustic ranch kitchen in a soft, yellow glow. To the left of the back door was a small storage closet where Darcy generally stashed her large animal box when it wasn't in the truck.

Darcy kept her supplies in a moderately-sized tackle box that served perfectly to organize her drugs and other small equipment. Olivia flipped open the lid and slid out the upper trays holding syringes, needles, and smaller items, to rummage through the bottom of the box where Darcy kept her injectable medications. She quickly found the flunixin bottle and plucked a twelve-cc syringe and eighteen-gauge needle from the tray. After drawing up the required dose of medication, she hurried back to the paddock.

"How did the vet say to give the injection?" she asked.

"He said it can either go intravenously or in the muscle. IV works faster."

She hesitated. "I'm not comfortable giving an IV injection. If I accidentally hit an artery, it could be disastrous. How about you?"

He shook his head. "No, I leave IVs to the professionals, if at all possible. Just give it in the muscle."

"Okay." The truth was, although she had extensive horse experience, she wasn't all that comfortable veering into medical territory, period. She took a long, slow breath, uncapped the syringe, and gave Dandy two sharp pats on his neck before plunging in the needle. Before injecting the contents of the syringe, she drew back on the plunger to ascertain she hadn't inadvertently hit a blood vessel. In the dwindling light, she had to strain to see, but it didn't appear any blood had been sucked into the barrel. She quickly administered the injection and withdrew the needle, capping the end, and dropping the whole thing into her pocket.

They eyed each other over the sick horse.

"I'm glad you're here," she said. "Thanks for staying with me."

He furrowed his brows. "Do you think I would leave you here to deal with this alone?"

She shrugged. "No, but I didn't know if you'd already gone home."

"Even if I had left, you know you can always call me for an emergency, don't you?"

Olivia nodded. "I guess it's just not come up before."

Cam clucked his tongue to Dandy, whose knees had started to buckle, and urged him to walk while they waited on the vet.

Although it seemed like forever, the headlights of Dr. Lockhart's truck shone at the turn into the driveway about thirty minutes later. He rambled up the long driveway and slid from his truck. Grabbing a large tackle box similar to Darcy's from his truck bed, he strode with determination toward the suffering animal. With a cursory greeting, he worked swiftly to evaluate the situation, repeating the steps Olivia had taken initially. The horizon rose to meet the sun, casting long shadows across the paddock as the competent doctor stuck his stethoscope into his ears and listened to first the horse's chest, then the belly.

Replacing the stethoscope around his neck, he said, "Decreased gut sounds. He may have an impaction."

Olivia and Cam watched as the vet pulled a plastic sleeve from his box and applied liberal lubrication.

"Is he likely to need restraint for rectal palpation?" asked the vet.

Olivia and Cam exchanged glances. "I don't think so," she finally said. "But if you'd like us to twitch him, we can."

"Just push him up against the gate and I'll see how he does."

They complied while the doctor proceeded with the examination. Dandy danced around a little but was overall compliant. All the while, Olivia uttered soft, reassuring words to the animal.

Dr. Lockhart removed his arm and pulled off the sleeve. "I don't feel anything, but you can only tell so much on palpation. Let me get the ultrasound."

They waited while the vet strode back to the truck, returning with a portable ultrasound unit. After powering up the machine, he applied jelly to the probe and scanned both sides of the horse's abdomen with swift, confident strokes. The tension in Olivia's neck and shoulders relaxed as the gentle hum of the ultrasound competed with the chirp of the evening insects and birds. The calm, competent manner in which the vet conducted the procedure reassured her. She glanced over at Cam, noting the worry lines between his brows had loosened.

Finally, the vet wiped the probe on his coveralls and moved the ultrasound outside of the paddock where it wouldn't inadvertently be damaged. Turning back to them, he said, "I don't see anything alarming, and it appears the flunixin has kicked in. Still, he seems a bit dehydrated. I'll give him some oral fluids which should help with hydration as well as gut motility."

Olivia let out a long, deep breath. "Then you don't think it's anything serious?"

The vet shook his head. "Not at this point. But I think someone should stay with him tonight just in case." He walked to his truck again, returning with a stainless-steel bucket, a stomach tube, a pump, and a bag of electrolyte powder.

Handing the bucket to Cam, he said, "Would you please fill this with a gallon of water?"

Cam walked briskly to the outdoor sink on the side of the barn and came back, water sloshing over the sides of the bucket in his haste.

Dr. Lockhart dumped the contents of his packet into the bucket and stirred with the end of the stomach pump. Then he lubricated the end of the stomach tube, reached across Dandy's nose, and inserted the tip into the ventral-medial aspect of the horse's left nostril. Dandy tossed his head in protest, dislodging the tube.

"I'm afraid we'll need the twitch," said the vet. "This is rather unpleasant."

Olivia raced to the barn, located the pole with the looped chain on the end, and dashed back to the paddock. With an experienced hand, she placed the chain over Dandy's upper lip and twisted. The twitch helped to calm the animal, as well as provide the necessary restraint for the procedure. She held onto the handle as the vet easily passed the stomach tube and ascertained it was placed properly.

"Easy, boy, it'll be over in a minute," she whispered.

Dr. Lockhart quickly administered the fluids, then kinked the tube to prevent fluid from leaking into the trachea as it was removed and eased it out.

Olivia unwound the chain and massaged Dandy's lip. "Good boy," she cooed. "This will make you feel better."

The vet gathered his equipment and headed back to the truck, Olivia on his heels.

"Thank you so much, doctor. I can't believe Darcy just left a few hours ago."

Dr. Lockhart chuckled as he stowed his gear. The bucket, with the tube and pump sticking out, clanged against the metallic truck bed as he tossed it over the side. "That's always the way things go. My animals always get sick or injured when I'm gone. Don't worry. I won't let anything happen to my colleague's horse. But seriously, if he should get worse, call me right away."

Olivia nodded, the relief palpable in her previously tight chest. She watched the truck back up and head down the long driveway, crunching gravel under its tires. When she turned to go back to where she'd left Cam with Dandy, she found he had already put the horse back in his stall.

Cam sat on a saddle pad just outside the open stall door, his back resting against a hay bale.

"Thanks, Cam, you can go. I'll stay with Dandy tonight."

He looked up at her and raised his eyebrows. "No. I'll stay. The ranch is my responsibility while Ben is away."

"But the horses—"

"Are also my responsibility. Besides, I'm not leaving you out here alone all night."

She clenched her jaw and thrust out her chin. "I've sat up with many sick horses by myself and I'm more than capable of—"

"I'm sure you are, but I'm *not* leaving you out here alone. End of discussion." The determination in his eyes said he meant business.

Olivia huffed. "Fine. Then I'm staying with you."

Cam released a weary sigh. "Suit yourself. Pull up a hay bale and have a seat." He leaned his head back and pulled his hat down over his eyes.

Part of Olivia wanted to take offense at his male chauvinism, the other part was grateful.

Chapter Eight

Cam woke to bright shards of sunlight hitting his face as they pierced through the center of the small, dirty window in the opposite side of the barn. He rubbed his stiff neck, then realized he couldn't move his legs. Just before panic drove the air from his lungs, he looked down and saw the reason. Olivia lay curled up in the fetal position next to him, her head across his thighs. He grinned.

At some point during the night, she had foraged through Ben and Darcy's cupboards and returned with snacks and a thermos of coffee. Later, as they'd kept their mostly silent vigil, a chill had settled in, and she'd rummaged up some old blankets from somewhere. Even though the blankets smelled of must and horse, and were a bit scratchy, they'd been a welcome respite from the cold. Still later, they'd both fallen asleep, and somehow, her head had ended up in his lap.

He had to give her credit for spunk. Tough and smart, Olivia could have stayed up with Dandy and handled any problems that might have arisen. Of that, he'd had no doubt. Still, he didn't feel right going off and leaving a young girl by herself at a lonely ranch. He knew his attitude had irritated her, but she'd just have to deal with it. His male protectiveness forbade him to do otherwise.

Cam tried to shift his legs, which had gone numb, but didn't want to wake her. They'd both been up late last night and both had to work today. Neither had slept well on the hard barn floor and prickly straw. He consulted his watch. Six-fifteen. His gaze shifted to the sick horse, relieved to see Dandy munching on hay, the grinding of his molars a reassuring sound. The animal appeared no worse for his experience. He'd probably had a more restful night than Cam and Olivia.

The slam of a vehicle door startled him, and he knew Ricky had arrived for work early. Suddenly, not wanting to be caught in this perfectly innocent, but to other people potentially questionable situation, he jostled his legs, waking Olivia.

She opened her eyes, a few seconds of confusion clouding her face, then her eyes went wide and she sat up, knocking over the thermos lying next to her. A deep blush crawled up her neck to her face.

Finding her embarrassment and the smidgeon of drool on his dusty jeans slightly amusing, he reached over and plucked a strand of hay from her tousled hair.

Obviously still disoriented, she stuttered, "I'm sorry. I didn't mean to fall asleep." She conveniently didn't mention not only falling asleep but ending up in his lap. Hopping to her feet, she took a step toward the stall. "Dandy—"

"Is fine, as you can see." Cam stretched his aching legs to restore circulation, then tucked his legs under him and rose, a bit wobbly as the blood returning to his lower extremities made them tingly. "I think he's over whatever ailed him."

She kept her eyes on the animal, and it occurred to him that he should alleviate this awkward situation by leaving. "I'm going to go wash up and see what I can rummage in the kitchen for breakfast. Are you hungry?"

She shook her head, still turned away from him, still red-faced.

"Okay. See you later."

He arched his back and massaged the kinks from his aching muscles as far as he could reach, then walked out of the barn into the bright sun. A chill still hung in the morning air, but the day would heat up quickly. A little foggy-headed from lack of sleep, as well as stiff from sitting on the barn floor against a hay bale, Cam realized his age was starting to catch up with him. It used to be he could pull all-nighters with nothing more than a nagging headache to show for it. Now, he didn't know how he was going to put one foot in front of the other. Coffee. He needed strong coffee and lots of it. He ran into Ricky coming out of the kitchen slurping his own coffee from an oversized mug. Cam shook his head. He didn't know how many times Ricky had spilled coffee because he could never find his thermos.

"Must've been quite a night," Ricky quipped. "You look like something the cat coughed up."

"Yeah, well, unlike some people who slept in a soft, warm bed last night, I slept in the barn with a sick horse." Cam brushed by him, the need for caffeine becoming more urgent by the second.

Ricky placed a hand on his arm. "Whoa, what're you talking about?"

Cam ran a weary hand over his stubbled face. "Dandy colicked last night."

"What? Why didn't you call me, man?" Concern replaced the teasing in Ricky's dark eyes.

"You'd already left."

"I would have come back and helped. No point in you doing everything by yourself."

Just then, Olivia wandered out of the barn like a sleepwalker. Ricky's gaze darted to her, taking in her appearance, then back to Cam, and a slow grin spread across his face.

"Oh, now I get it."

Cam blew out a disgusted breath. "You get *what*, exactly?"

"Two's company, three's—"

Cam's lips flattened. "Don't go there, professor. Olivia was dealing with Dandy all by herself when I finished up. I couldn't leave her to handle a sick horse alone." He knew it annoyed Ricky when he called him "professor," but right now, he felt like annoying Ricky. He hoped his burning eyes conveyed the message to drop the conversation right now. Or maybe the burning was merely due to a lack of sleep and his eyes weren't projecting the fiery darts he thought they were.

But Ricky apparently got the message because he changed the subject. "Is Dandy okay?"

"Yeah. He seems fine this morning. We called Dr. Lockhart."

Ricky slapped him on the back. "Good. You want to take the day off, get some sleep?"

Cam shook his head. "Can't. With Ben gone, there's too much to do. But I'm sure feeling my age today."

"You want me to get you some coffee?"

Cam almost laughed. This was Ricky's attempt to make up for his earlier teasing. "Thanks, but I'll get it. I'm going to rustle up something for breakfast, too. I'll join you in a few minutes."

"Take your time." Ricky took another swig of his coffee and ambled toward the barn.

~

Olivia passed Ricky on her way to the house, and the heat rose in her face again. He tipped his hat at her, but she averted her eyes. It was mortifying enough that she'd somehow managed to lay her head in Cam's lap. The last thing she needed was for gossip to get started. She didn't know how she was going to face Cam this morning, but she really needed to use the bathroom and clean up in the house. There was no time to go home and get back in time for her first lesson. Plus, her stomach reminded her they hadn't eaten a proper dinner last night, as it complained loudly.

She pushed open the door to the kitchen and found Cam scrambling eggs. The wonderful aroma emanating from the stove caused her belly to rumble. Great, just great. Not only had she embarrassed herself by lying in such an intimate way with a man she barely knew, but now her body was betraying her with unladylike noises. She prayed he hadn't heard her stomach growling over the sizzling of the frying pan.

With his back to her, he asked, "Did you change your mind about breakfast?"

Her voice caught in her throat, still burning with humiliation. "Um . . . yeah, I could eat." But the moment the words left her mouth, she didn't know how she would manage to move the food down her constricted throat to her anxiously awaiting stomach.

"Okay. If you want to wash up, I'll toss in another couple of eggs. There's fresh coffee, too, if you want some."

"Thanks." She fled to the bathroom, where she washed her face and did her best to detangle her wild hair. When she returned to the kitchen, she saw that Cam had generously served up two plates of eggs and toast and poured her a cup of coffee.

"I don't know how you take your coffee, other than out of a thermos late at night."

"Oh. Usually with cream and sugar." She reached for the creamer and sugar bowl in the center of the table and stirred a generous amount of each into her mug. "Wow, this looks good." She bowed her head and said a short, silent prayer, feeling a little conspicuous. She didn't know Cam's religious convictions, if any.

"I already blessed the food, but a double blessing can't hurt, even if I'm a pretty good cook." He grinned at her and picked up his fork. "But, then again, it's hard to mess up eggs and toast."

"Oh." Why couldn't she think of something more intelligent to say? She tried to return his smile but feared her face contorted more into a grimace. Why did she feel so awkward this morning? Although they hadn't talked much last night, they'd passed the hours in companionable silence. *Just eat your breakfast, Olivia.* She shoved a bite of egg in her mouth to keep it occupied. "Mm, this is really good."

Cam chuckled. "Nah, you're just hungry. You gonna be okay today?"

His eyes took in her haggard appearance, and she couldn't help wondering how the woman who sat across from him compared to the one he'd danced with at the wedding. At least he knew she was capable of looking better than she did at this minute. Not that it mattered. She didn't particularly care one way or the other what Cam thought about her looks. She wasn't out to impress him. Olivia was a what-you-see-is-what-you-get kind of girl. Still, she didn't like the idea that he might be repulsed by her worn-out presentation, not to mention the fact she'd slept with her head in his lap. She felt the heat rise to her face again, and she quickly picked up her toast to partially block his view.

"Yeah, I'll be fine. I have a class in thirty minutes, so I don't have much choice." Then she allowed herself to study his face, which looked as tired as hers, only covered with dark whiskers. "How about you? Are you going to be able to work today?" It suddenly occurred to her that his job involved enough danger without being physically and mentally impaired.

He took a long sip of coffee. "Now that I've had caffeine, I'm good to go."

He smiled over the brim of his cup, and it struck her that he had a nice smile. She'd never noticed it before. Cam wasn't a particularly handsome man in the same way that Kyle was, but he had a rugged, honest face.

She must have let her gaze linger a little too long, for he said, "What? Do I look *that* bad? And, by the way, are you going to eat that toast?"

"What?" She looked at the toast she had been holding for the last couple of minutes without taking a bite. "Oh, yeah." She chewed off a corner and, with her mouth full, said, "No, you don't look bad. Probably not as bad as I do."

"I wouldn't worry about it. You're young. You can get away with all-nighters. Me, I feel older by the minute." He rose and carried his dishes to the sink. Then, retrieving his hat from the peg by the door, he said, "Thanks for the company last night. Be careful today."

Olivia swallowed her bite of toast and replied, "You, too." She quickly finished the rest of her breakfast and, carrying her own plate to the sink, realized he'd left her to do the dishes. "Typical man." But rather than feeling irritated, she found his action amusing as she reached for the dish soap.

Chapter Nine

Cam couldn't help worrying about Olivia as he went about his work. He didn't know why—he'd never worried about her before. Grinning, he had to admire her determination to stay last night and, truth be known, he'd welcomed her company. She was the real deal, a good kid. No, not a kid. A responsible, intelligent, hard-working young woman who loved her job working with horses as much as he did ranching. The low pay didn't matter as long as they were doing what they loved best. If he were ever to find a compatible partner, for which he was most assuredly *not* looking, it would have to be someone like Olivia. Not Olivia, of course. He was too old for her. But it seemed the women he'd dated had never quite measured up to the ideal woman he had in his mind. Perhaps that was because he'd never completely defined what it was he wanted in a wife. Besides, he was perfectly content being single. He'd been on his own most of his life and fully expected to remain that way.

He wasn't like Ben, who'd suffered a broken engagement, or Ricky, whose first wife had died tragically in a botched mugging. Both of them had dealt with heartache and pain before finding the love of their life. Cam claimed no dramatic past to put him off of marriage, per se, but some men just weren't cut out to be married. So why was he thinking about marriage all of a sudden? It must be the lack of sleep or the fact that life at the ranch had drastically changed with both Ben and Ricky tying the knot. Something akin to loss settled in his chest as he remembered life when it was just the three of them—the three amigos—before women entered the picture. He chided himself for his wayward thoughts. He didn't begrudge Ben and Ricky for finding happiness. Sometimes stress and fatigue made a person act and think in ways they wouldn't under ordinary circumstances.

Cam shook his head to clear it and tried to focus on the black Angus cattle grazing on the hillside. They did twice-a-day checks to be sure the animals looked healthy and were safe. The creatures barely gave him notice as he rode slowly around the herd, searching for any irregularity. Several cows nursed calves, and several more cows would be calving soon. It was imperative to catch any problems early on to prevent complications.

Spring was Cam's favorite time of year, not only in bringing relief from the frigid winter temperatures but in the renewal of life everywhere he looked. The earthy smell of the pastures regenerating with an abundance of green grass, providing fresh grazing for the cattle, was more intoxicating to Cam than just about anything in the world, and although calving season meant extra work, he never tired of seeing new life. Soon they would be vaccinating, deworming, and placing ear tags for identification. The workdays would be long, but with increasing daylight, more doable. The sun had chased away the earlier chill, bringing welcome warmth to the day. Raising his tired eyes to the budding trees, he smiled at the new life emerging all around, another of God's wonders. Wildflowers fearlessly poked their heads through the thawed soil, taking a chance an unexpected snowstorm wouldn't come along. Spring in Wyoming was finicky like that, waffling between reverting back to winter and plowing full speed ahead toward summer. It wasn't uncommon for one day to be warm enough to tease people into thinking the cold days were finally behind them, then dumping a foot of snow the next day.

As the day wound down, Cam headed back to the barn, ready to go home and fall into bed. He might not even take off his boots. Not surprisingly, he saw Olivia still at work, leading the last horse from her trail ride into the barn. She'd put in a long day, too.

He dismounted and let Malachi graze for a few minutes, then leaned over and grabbed a saddle that Olivia had left on the ground just outside the paddock. They bumped into each other as she returned to the paddock.

"You forgot something," he said.

She frowned. "I was coming back for the saddle," she said, her tone defensive.

"I know. I thought I'd save you some steps." He continued to the tack room.

Olivia reversed course and followed him. "You didn't have to do that."

He deposited the saddle on the rack. "I know that, too. I was only trying to help." Reaching for a cleaning rag hanging on a hook, he began wiping down the saddle.

Her hands rested on her hips and her eyes narrowed. "Why? Why are you being so nice to me all of a sudden?"

Cam turned toward her, his palms up. "I didn't realize I was suddenly being nice. Here I thought I'd always been a nice guy." At her still skeptical expression, he continued. "Look, I know you're exhausted. I assure you I don't have any ulterior motives, like stealing your job."

Her shoulders relaxed. "I'm sorry. I should have just said thank you."

"You're welcome. You go on home and I'll finish up in here."

She nodded. "Thanks. And Cam?"

He looked up. "Yes?"

She grinned. "You really are a nice guy. Except for leaving me with the breakfast dishes."

His hand flew to his forehead. "I completely forgot. I didn't do it on purpose."

"I'm not sure I buy your excuse, but I'll give you the benefit of the doubt." Then, without warning, she raised on tiptoe and kissed his cheek.

He stared at her, wide-eyed. It appeared she'd shocked herself as much as she'd shocked him. Without another word, she turned and fled from the barn.

~

What did you just do? What were you thinking? Olivia berated herself all the way to her car, where she jumped inside and peeled down the driveway, spewing pebbles in her wake. What was wrong with her, anyway? *Kissing* him? What had possessed her? She tried to justify her action in her mind but came up blank. It had to be the exhaustion. Suddenly a man performed an act of kindness for her and she fell apart.

And Cam putting away her saddle *had* been an act of kindness, nothing more. He'd been nice enough to stay with her all through last night. He'd even cooked her breakfast this morning. He'd danced with her out of pity at the wedding. Her face flamed with shame. If she weren't careful, she could easily transfer her suppressed feelings for Kyle to the first nice man who came along, namely Cam. It didn't matter how nicely he treated her, he was a colleague. Period. One who was probably appalled at her display of affection on top of using him as a human pillow. The surprise on his face told her that much. He would probably make efforts to avoid being alone with her ever again.

She would not, under any circumstances, allow such an inappropriate action to repeat itself. She would save Cam the trouble and avoid him first before he had to resort to avoiding her.

Chapter Ten

Two weeks had gone by since the ill-advised kiss. Olivia took care to stay away from Cam to the point of ducking out of sight when he happened to walk by. One morning she hid behind a haystack when he came into the barn before she could exit.

"What are you doing?"

Darcy's voice made Olivia jump.

"Oh, I . . . didn't hear you come in. I . . . I thought I dropped something." Olivia stood upright, her lie unconvincing even to herself.

Darcy shot a look over her shoulder at Cam opening Kimber's stall and scrunched her eyes. "What?" She crossed her arms over her chest. "What did you drop?"

Olivia's mouth went dry. *Think of something. Quickly.* "Oh, um . . . my pen. But it was right here in my pocket." She extracted the pen from her vest pocket and held it up for Darcy's inspection, attempting a smile.

Darcy waited until Cam had led the gelding out to the paddock. "Did something happen between you and Cam?"

Olivia felt the blood drain from her face, and she averted her eyes. "Of course not. What are you talking about?"

Her friend drew in a long breath and leveled her gaze on Olivia. She could feel Darcy's piercing eyes on her even though she hadn't raised her own eyes from something fascinating on the barn floor.

"Ever since the night Dandy colicked, you've been acting weird around him. Did anything happen that night that I should know about?"

"No!" Olivia's voice came out higher and more strident than she'd intended. "No, he was a perfect gentleman. I was grateful I didn't have to spend the night alone with Dandy." *I'm the one who lost my head.*

"Then why—"

Darcy's question was cut short by the ringing of Olivia's phone. *Thank you, God.* She glanced at the caller ID but didn't recognize the number. "Excuse me." She turned her back to Darcy who, fortunately, took the hint and left. "Hello?"

"Is this Olivia?" came a soft voice through the receiver.

"Yes. Who's this?" Olivia sat on the hay bale she'd hidden behind, scootching over from a pricky piece of straw sticking out the top.

A long pause ensued. "This is Martha."

Olivia's brow knitted as she tried to recall someone by that name.

"Your sister."

Olivia's heart stuttered to a stop, then began pounding. "Martha?" She hadn't seen her half-sister in over twenty years. Not since she'd been a small child.

It sounded like the other woman was crying, and

it took several long seconds before she spoke again. "I apologize for calling out of the blue. I didn't have any other option."

Olivia waited, half angry at the woman who'd put her firmly out of her life, and half wondering what had made her reach out now.

When she didn't respond, Martha continued in a shaky voice. "I need your help, Olivia. You're my only living relative."

"What kind of help?" Wariness colored Olivia's tone. "Money? Because if that's what you need, I don't have—"

"No, not money." A long sigh followed.

"Then what?" Whatever Martha wanted, it had to be big. Whatever it was, Olivia was also sure she didn't want to be involved. She'd lived perfectly fine without her half-sister in her life and there was no reason to get dragged down into whatever trouble Martha was in. "Look, I—"

"I'm asking you to take my son." The words spilled out in a breathless rush.

Olivia's heart flip-flopped against her ribs. Son? She had a nephew she'd never known about? Not that it mattered. She'd never had a relationship with Martha, let alone her half-sister's family. The impact of what Martha had just said failed to reach the logical part of her brain. This had to be some sort of joke or something.

"I'm dying, Oliva. There's nobody else."

The conversation had just gone from weird to insane. Was Martha actually asking her to raise her kid? A kid she'd never seen? Why *her*? Martha knew nothing about Olivia. Olivia could be a drug dealer or a child abuser for all Martha knew about her. This couldn't possibly be for real.

Olivia barked out a mirthless laugh. "You don't even know me. Surely there is somebody closer to you, a friend or, what about the boy's father?"

Martha hesitated. "It's complicated."

Without meaning to, Olivia blurted out, "I'll bet it is." This was the most bizarre conversation she'd ever had. "Look, Martha, you can't just call me up after twenty years and dump this news on me. I'm sorry about your situation but I can't take care of a kid. I can barely take care of myself." She hated admitting it, but her last words were true. She lived in a tiny apartment and lived paycheck to paycheck.

More sobbing at the other end of the phone. "Olivia, would you please do just one thing for me?"

"I don't know. It depends on what it is."

"Would you please come visit me? I'd like to see you before . . ."

Olivia almost said, "Why, after twenty years?" But she pulled the words back before they left her mouth. People sometimes did odd things when they knew they were dying, like wanting closure with estranged relatives. She supposed she should feel something other than aggravation, but the truth was she didn't feel anything toward Martha. They were total strangers. No sadness pricked her heart any more than it would for anyone else she didn't know.

"Look, I don't even know where you live—"

"Utah, just outside of Salt Lake City."

"And I can't just take off work—"

"I'll take care of your plane ticket and reimburse you for your time off."

Olivia drew a deep breath through her nose and blew it out slowly. "I'll have to think about it. I'll call you tomorrow."

Sniffling sounded in her ear. "Thank you. I'm sorry for not keeping in contact, Olivia. I really am."

Yeah, me too. It occurred to Olivia that she could have just as easily reached out to Martha now that she was an adult, but there'd been no reason. Not that she would have known where to find her. For that matter, Olivia wondered how Martha had gotten her phone number. But that was a question for another day.

"Okay, I'll call you tomorrow," she repeated.

~

"I didn't know you had a sister," said Darcy. She perched on the top porch step her arms wrapped around her knees, her attention focused on Olivia.

"For most of my life, neither did I." Olivia pushed her legs against the floorboards of the porch and set the swing she rested on into motion. She appreciated Darcy, who was so much more than her employer. Whenever she needed to talk, Darcy was always a willing listener. She'd immediately stopped what she was doing and suggested they sit on the front porch where they would be unlikely to be disturbed. She'd even poured them each a large glass of lemonade.

"I mean, I knew Martha existed, but we never had any kind of relationship." Olivia tucked a stray strand of hair that had escaped her ponytail behind her ear. "It's a rather sordid story."

Darcy gave her a sympathetic smile, encouraging her to go on.

Olivia pulled in a breath and blurted out the truth. "My dad left Martha and her mom to marry my mom.

He waited until Martha was out of high school, but he and my mom had been having an affair for a couple of years while he was still married to Martha's mom." She didn't know why admitting that fact made her feel dirty. It wasn't as though *she'd* had anything to do with the whole mess. "I was born a few months after Mom and Dad married."

Darcy fiddled with her wedding ring, twisting it back and forth across her finger. "So, Martha understandably resented you."

Olivia shrugged. "I suppose. I never particularly thought about it until she called—how she must have felt, I mean. I only saw her a couple of times when I was little. She came to visit twice, as I recall, but the only thing I remember is her and Mom and Dad yelling a lot. I thought it was kind of neat having a grown-up big sister. But I don't remember her paying much attention to me."

The sound of horses' hooves came from behind the house, announcing the men returning from the pastures. Olivia's head swiveled to the sound, but she knew they'd be a while putting the horses and tack away. Besides, they were unlikely to interrupt two women in the middle of a heart-to-heart. No man wanted to get drawn into female drama. Still, just in case they did decide to join the women, she didn't particularly want to air her family's dirty laundry in front of everyone. Darcy could tell Ben later.

"Don't worry about them," Darcy said, apparently reading Olivia's thoughts. She urged her to continue. "Is that why Martha stopped visiting? Because she and your dad fought?"

Olivia shook her head. "Dad died when I was

four. There was no reason for her to continue to come. I'm sure she couldn't stand the sight of my mother, since Martha and her mom blamed my mom for breaking up their family."

A nippy breeze stirred the late afternoon air, making the wind chimes hanging above the porch sing. Olivia wrapped her arms around herself.

"Are you cold? Do you want a sweater?" asked Darcy. The descending sun sent slanted rays against the steps, painting the wood in warm shades of gold.

"No, I'll move into the sun." Olivia rose from the swing and settled on the step next to Darcy. She took a sip of her lemonade, enjoying the heat from the boards beneath her and the soothing tinkling of the wind chimes. "I never met Martha's mother, but I understand she was bitter about the divorce until she died a few years ago."

"So, Martha really doesn't have any other family? Where's the boy's father?"

Olivia laughed. "Sperm donor. Martha never married and she was getting older and wanted a child."

Darcy smiled. "The wonders of modern medicine. How old is her son?"

"Four. The same age I was when Dad died." Olivia's brow furrowed. "While she was pregnant, she developed breast cancer. She refused chemotherapy until after Brian was born. By then, it had become more advanced, but she managed to fight it for four years. It's a miracle she's survived this long."

Darcy nodded. "The struggle to survive becomes more urgent when you have another person to think about."

"I want to dislike her, Darcy, but I'm finding

myself feeling sorry for her. Plus, part of me is curious to meet her."

"It sounds like a good idea. If you don't, you might regret it later." She scooted closer and laid her hand on Olivia's arm.

Olivia bit her lip and spoke softly. "But I can't take her kid."

Darcy squeezed Olivia's arm. "Have you prayed about it?"

Olivia frowned. "No, I don't need to. I know I'm not cut out to raise a kid by myself. You've seen my little apartment. You know how much money I make." She realized her last statement could be construed as complaining about her salary. "I didn't mean that to sound like—"

"I understand." Darcy laughed. "But Ben and I were talking, and since Whispering Winds Trail Rides has been open, we've been doing well, largely thanks to you. We discussed giving you a raise."

Olivia's mouth opened and she shook her head. "Darcy, I never meant to imply—"

"Stop. You've earned it. As for the other matter, why don't you give it to God? His plans are always best."

"Okay." Olivia reluctantly agreed, but she knew God would never expect her to be a single parent to her nephew.

Chapter Eleven

"Where's the cowgirl been? Haven't seen her for a few days," said Ricky. The three men worked together placing ear tags on the new calves, with one restraining, one tagging, and one recording the number. The work needed to get done before the calves got too big to restrain manually and they had to use a cow chute. Ricky had snagged the sweet job of recording while Ben and Cam sweated with the physical labor.

"Visiting her sister in Utah," said Ben, as he placed the ear tag gun against the middle part of the left ear of a bawling calf held firmly against Cam's thighs. Ben squeezed the gun, verified the male tab went all the way through the hole in the tag, and stepped back.

Cam released the offended animal, who took off without a backward glance, and wiped his brow with the back of his gloved hand. Now that he thought about it, he realized he hadn't seen Olivia, either. Not that he'd been looking for her.

"Didn't know she had a sister," said Ricky.

Ben pulled another tag from the box and rattled the number off to Ricky. "Yeah, a half-sister, actually. They haven't seen each other in twenty years. Then a few days ago, she called Olivia and told her she was dying."

"Yikes. What a bummer." Ricky stuck his pencil in his jacket pocket. "How 'bout that one right over there?" He pointed to a calf several feet away.

Cam reached up and massaged a throbbing shoulder. "How about *you* take a turn rounding up calves and *I* play secretary for a while?"

Ricky grinned. "I was wondering when you were going to start complaining." He handed the clipboard to Cam and he and Ben converged on an unsuspecting animal.

Cam reached for his water bottle and took a long swallow. The talk about Olivia took him back to the night after the colic when she'd kissed his cheek. He shut out the cacophony of bellowing cattle and the grunting of the other two men chasing after them, as the memory of that unexpected kiss replayed in his mind. They had both been somewhat loopy with fatigue, and she had gone from questioning him about why he was helping her put away her saddle to teasing him about leaving her with dirty breakfast dishes. The next thing he knew, he'd felt the brush of her lips and the warmth of her breath against his face. Then she'd stepped back, seeming as surprised as he was, and fled. The sensation of the brief encounter lingered on his cheek like a weak flame. In the days that followed, he'd wondered what her action had meant. Was it simply an impulsive act, one to which she had given no thought, or perhaps one she now regretted, or had it meant more? Did she perhaps have feelings for him?

What would he think of the idea if she *did* have feelings for him? That would certainly be a dilemma.

The possibility that she could be using him as a Kyle substitute had to be considered, and he didn't want to be anyone's rebound. But suppose she'd suddenly taken notice of him like he had her? He had to admit he hadn't paid much attention to Olivia before the wedding or Dandy's colic, so he couldn't say how often their paths had crossed in the past as they went about their work on the ranch. But somehow, that seemingly innocent little kiss had left a mark on him. He didn't want to read too much into it, but he couldn't stop thinking about it, or her. How *did* he feel about her?

He found himself caught in a confusing contrast of emotions. On one hand, he'd always admired Olivia's work ethic and ability and found her to be a capable colleague at the ranch. And recently, he'd glimpsed the more vulnerable, feminine side of her—not only sweet and genuine but stunningly attractive. Should he take the risk of venturing out of his comfort zone to explore more? His other hand told him he was being foolish and she didn't care any more for him than she would a big brother. He had never had an overwhelming urge to be paired up with a woman, so why should he leave the comfort and safety of his familiar routine? He struggled with the uncertainty and apprehension of his conflicting thoughts, and he didn't like it. Why not leave well enough alone?

Besides, it almost seemed as though she had been avoiding him since that night. Or was it just his imagination? Maybe he had just become more focused on her whereabouts, purposefully looking for her. He shook his head, willing the clashing thoughts to vanish. This was exactly why he'd had no intention of getting tangled up with a woman. A man couldn't keep his head on straight. His thoughts betrayed him by returning to the night of the wedding when he'd held her in his arms, feeling her softness against him, and inhaling the scent of her silky hair. Man, that experience had been nice.

Cam dropped the clipboard to the ground and put his hands to his temples, trying to force out the memories that didn't mean a thing. Why would she be attracted to him? What was there about him to attract an amazing young woman like Olivia? A simple man, Cam had no advanced college degree or ambition to be anything more than what he was, a lowly ranch hand. His appearance, although not repulsive, was merely average. He didn't have Ben or Ricky's dark good looks. Then there was his age. Surely, if Olivia knew what he was thinking, she would laugh at him for making such a preposterous presumption. He'd better derail this conversation in his head before any of it left his mouth and made him look like a bigger fool than he was.

"What are you meditating about?" Ricky's joking voice jolted Cam back to the present. They were in the middle of a large pasture with potentially dangerous animals doing potentially dangerous work. He needed to keep his wits about him.

"Nothing. Just a little headache." He bent to retrieve his clipboard and forced himself to focus on the job at hand.

~

Later that evening, Cam got to thinking about what he'd heard about Olivia's sister. Olivia had to be going through a tough time. Maybe he should call her to just . . . just what? It wasn't like they were best friends. She must have close friends she could talk to if she needed a sympathetic ear or help with anything. Like Darcy, for instance. But still, it might encourage her to hear a friendly voice. That's all. He shouldn't just ignore this difficulty in her life as though he didn't care.

Before he lost his nerve, Cam reached for his cell and scrolled down his list of contacts until he found her name. The realization hit him that he'd never called her before. He only had her number because he had all the numbers of the people at the ranch.

"You're checking on a friend who's dealing with a problem, nothing more," he told himself, as he hit the call button.

"Hello?"

At the sound of her voice, the back of his throat tightened and he couldn't force out a sound.

"Hello? Cam? Is that you?"

Caller ID. Busted. "Yeah," he croaked. He cleared his throat and tried again. "I heard about your sister. I just wanted to say how sorry I am."

"Thanks."

She wasn't going to make this easy for him. "Well, if there's anything I can do . . ." Why did people always say, "If there's anything I can do" when they knew perfectly well there wasn't? What could he possibly do for her or her dying sister? Still, it seemed like the right thing to say.

A sigh reached his ear. "Thanks, I appreciate it. But there's nothing I need right now."

A long silence stretched between them, filling the air with tension. "Okay, well, I just wanted to let you know I was thinking of you."

"Thanks. It was nice of you to call."

"Okay, well, see you when you get back."

"Yeah, see you. Bye." The call disconnected.

Well, that had certainly been awkward. Had he overstepped his bounds in presuming they were more than mere coworkers? No, certainly not. Coworkers still cared about each other, right? Once she returned, he would make an effort to be nice, but not overly so, so she wouldn't think he was being *too* friendly, and make her uncomfortable.

Chapter Twelve

Olivia swiped the phone off and smiled. How sweet of Cam to call. She'd been so concerned that she'd made an idiot of herself kissing him that he'd stay as far away from her as possible. But if that were true, he certainly wouldn't have called her. It was true what she'd told him. He was a nice guy. Maybe even more than a nice guy. But she couldn't let her thoughts go down that road. Not tonight.

Olivia placed the phone on her nightstand and lay on her bed, reliving the short time she'd been with Martha. Her sister had gone to bed over an hour ago, the exhaustion of the visit evident in her frail body. The couple of days since Olivia had arrived had been bittersweet. She had decided to drive the five hours to Martha's place rather than fly so she could have the extra time alone to mentally prepare herself. Not knowing what to expect, she'd been shocked to find an emaciated woman with sunken cheekbones and a pasty complexion. But Martha had perked up immediately upon seeing her, throwing her bony arms around Olivia's neck and greeting her warmly.

After Martha poured each of them a large glass of

iced tea, they sat in the living room of her small townhouse. The curtains had been pulled back, letting in beams of unfiltered sunlight that added to the warmth in the overheated room. Despite the heat, Martha wore sweats and sat bundled up in a blanket on the sofa. She had wrapped a colorful scarf around her head, which Olivia assumed covered her baldness. She motioned for Olivia to sit in the matching chair next to her where she gripped Olivia's hand in her thin, icy one.

Tears pooled in Martha's eyes. "I can't tell you how grateful I am that you came. I wouldn't have blamed you if you hadn't."

Despite her earlier misgivings, Olivia found herself drawn to her sister. She wasn't anything like Olivia remembered, but the years and Martha's disease had changed her appearance considerably. Besides, childhood memories were not always reliable.

Olivia smiled. "I had to come."

Martha blinked rapidly, clearing the tears, and spoke softly. "Olivia, I'm asking your forgiveness for the years I've wasted by not keeping in contact with you."

Olivia squeezed her hand. "It's perfectly understandable. What you and your mother went through because of—"

Martha shook her head. "Not because of you. You had nothing to do with any of it. You were an innocent child and I shouldn't have held a grudge against you for something that was not your fault."

A lump lodged in Olivia's throat at the admission, and she felt her own eyes beginning to sting with tears. "But I was a reminder of what Dad had done," she whispered.

The tears fell freely from Martha's eyes now, and she made no effort to wipe them away. "I'm afraid I allowed Mama's bitterness to rub off on me. I mean, yes, I was angry at the time. Even though I was technically an adult, I felt like my father had deserted me. I still needed my daddy. Then when you were born, it seemed like he had replaced me with a new child."

Olivia's heart squeezed with Martha's raw pain. "I'm so sorry. I should have realized—"

Martha shook her head again. "How could you? You were a child."

Tendrils of guilt wrapped themselves around Olivia's insides. "I'm not a child anymore. I should have reached out to you."

Letting go of Olivia's hand, Martha fished for a tissue in her pocket and wiped her face. It made no difference as the tears continued to flow unabated. "You had no reason to. I'd never made the effort to establish a relationship with you. *I'm* to blame, not you."

Olivia's lips trembled. "It doesn't matter now."

Martha's eyes widened and she snatched Olivia's hand once again with a surprisingly strong grip. "Yes, yes it does! I . . . I need you to know how much I regret . . . everything." She took a halting breath and continued. "Mama poisoned me against you and your mother, but I was a willing vessel. I suppose, deep down, I felt I would be disloyal to her if I maintained contact with Daddy's second family." She huffed out a sad laugh. "And, no doubt, she would have disowned me. But when she died five years ago, I still didn't make the effort because I thought, by that time, it was too late."

"It's okay. I understand. What Dad did hurt everyone." Olivia started to reach for her iced tea, but it sat too far away to get to without disengaging Martha's hand. She didn't want to break the contact, so she leaned back in her seat.

Martha didn't seem to notice, as she took a long drink from her own glass and wiped her hand across her mouth. "It's easy to blame everything on him, but the truth is Mom was a difficult person to live with. As long as I can remember, they were always fighting. He told me he only stayed with Mom until I graduated from high school." She sniffled and brought her rumpled tissue to her nose. "I don't condone his affair, but I have to admit your mother made him happy. I could see the change in him when I visited, although I didn't want to acknowledge it. I still felt like he'd left *me*, not Mom. But I noticed how the tension on his face disappeared, and he even joked and laughed."

Olivia sighed, a longing she couldn't describe washing over her. "I don't remember much about him."

Martha's eyes lit up, shimmering with unshed tears. "I can tell you lots of stories. Oh! And I have pictures." She hopped up and crossed the room to a bookshelf, where several photo albums stood packed together in the tight space. Pulling out a couple, she returned to the sofa and thumbed through the pages.

Olivia bent closer to inspect the faded pictures. A whole new world opened up to her as Martha lovingly pointed out people and places, describing in detail the man Olivia had known for such a brief time. Although she had some photos of her father, she really couldn't remember him. Listening to Martha's animated accounts, her father came alive in ways she'd never known. He'd been a good man, a good father, a person who had put up with years of verbal and emotional abuse before finally finding happiness. Perhaps his timing could have been better, but she couldn't fault him too much. He had stayed in his miserable first marriage until Martha was on her own.

Hours passed as Martha reminisced and Olivia eagerly soaked up information about her family while they poured over the albums. She'd barely noticed the loss of the sun as dusk rapidly approached until Martha rose to turn on the table lamps. A dull ache lodged in Olivia's chest at the fact that although she'd finally reconnected with Martha, their time together was short.

Martha closed the last album and set it on the coffee table atop several others. "Gracious, I've talked your ear off. You must be yawning with boredom."

"Not at all. I appreciate you telling me about . . ." she started to say, "Your family," then rethought her words and said, "Our family."

The iced tea long consumed, Olivia picked up her glass to take to the kitchen. "Can I get you more to drink?"

"No, thanks." Martha's energy seemed to have leached out of her body, and she sank back against the couch pillows.

Olivia's stomach growled, and she pressed a hand to her belly.

"Oh, I'm sorry. You must be starved." Martha started to rise, but Olivia stopped her.

"Please, let me fix dinner. You just rest."

Martha hesitated, then nodded. "I feel like a terrible hostess making my guest cook."

Olivia sat back down and took Martha's hand.

"I'm not a guest. I'm your sister." At Martha's smile, she said, "What would you like me to make?"

Martha sighed. "To be honest, I don't have much of an appetite these days. But I do have a few cans of soup and some sandwich fixings if you don't mind something simple."

Olivia grinned. "Simple is my specialty."

She carried the two glasses to the kitchen and rummaged around until she found the items she needed. In the few minutes it took to prepare dinner, Martha had fallen asleep. Olivia debated about whether or not to wake her, then decided to let her rest. If she woke later, Olivia could always reheat the soup, and the sandwich would keep.

She threw a blanket over the thin woman who looked even more fragile in sleep. Olivia should not have let her wear herself out by talking for so long. But Martha had seemed to enjoy it. With the long evening ahead of her, Olivia sat at the kitchen table and ate by herself. She should call or text some of her friends back home, but she didn't want to talk to anyone. She wanted to savor the time she'd spent with Martha and the history she'd discovered about her family. But the one topic Martha hadn't touched on was her son. Where was he and did Martha still expect Olivia to take him?

~

Olivia awoke to the smell of frying bacon. She glanced at her watch on the bedside table. Seven a.m. She didn't know what time she'd finally fallen asleep, but it was well past midnight. With so many revelations yesterday, thoughts churned through her mind, making sleep impossible. After her father died, her mother hadn't made an effort to keep any sort of connection with Martha, nor had she encouraged Olivia to do so. As Olivia grew older, she seldom thought of her half-sister. The fault for the estrangement ran both ways, to the detriment of both her father's daughters.

She pulled on a robe, shoved her feet into slippers, and made her way to the kitchen where Martha stood before the stove turning bacon with a fork.

"I apologize for falling asleep on you last night." Martha spoke with her back to Olivia as she flipped pancakes in another pan. "I imagine you're hungry this morning after the skimpy dinner you had to make for yourself."

"Martha, you didn't have to go to all this trouble. I would have taken you out to breakfast."

"Nonsense. I don't sleep all that well, so I'm usually up early. Morning is when my energy level is the highest. The least I can do is feed you." She smiled over her shoulder.

"What can I do to help?"

"Pour some juice and find the butter. Everything's almost ready."

They sat at the table in the cheerful kitchen with sunny, yellow walls and frilly white curtains. A refreshing breeze drifted in through the window above the sink, fluttering the curtains.

"Do you mind if I say grace?" Martha asked.

"No, of course not." After Martha had uttered a brief prayer ending, "In Jesus' name," Olivia said, "I'm glad to see you're a Christian." She refrained from adding that with what Martha was facing, she needed to be sure of her eternity.

Martha's face reddened. "Yeah, well that's another part of my life that I'm ashamed to say I took my sweet time about. I spent most of my life running from God, and things didn't exactly work out well." A sad smile touched her lips. "I finally stopped running and accepted Jesus as my Lord and Savior when I moved out here to undergo experimental treatment at a Christian-based cancer center in Salt Lake City. I needed the spiritual healing more than the physical. Although the cancer treatment didn't work, I gained something much better—the assurance of Heaven when I die."

Olivia's throat constricted with grief at finally finding her sister only to lose her. She sipped her orange juice which burned its way to her stomach.

Martha reached across the table and squeezed Olivia's hand. "Don't look so sad. I'm at peace about everything but Brian."

"Speaking of whom, where is he?"

"He spent yesterday and last night at a friend's house so we could have some time alone. He'll be home later this morning. I can't wait for you to meet him." Martha slathered butter on her pancakes and took a small bite.

Olivia's pulse kicked up a notch. Reconnecting with Martha was one thing. Raising her child was something else entirely. "Look, Martha, about Brian—"

Martha held up a hand. "I'm not asking you to take him. That's not why I wanted to see you. I shouldn't have sprung that request on you over the phone."

"But I thought . . . What will you do about him?"

Martha nibbled on a piece of bacon, her eyes fixed on something Olivia couldn't see. "I don't know. But I trust God has an answer."

Olivia swallowed her guilt for being inadequate to do the one thing her sister needed most. The guilt lay like a soggy lump in her stomach, making it difficult for her to eat the delicious breakfast Martha had taken the trouble to prepare.

Martha openly talked about her long journey with cancer, starting with when she was pregnant with Brian. "The doctors wanted me to abort him and start chemo right away. But I couldn't. I'd waited so long to be a mother, but the right man never came along. I don't regret my decision for one moment."

Olivia's admiration for her sister deepened. "You're a brave, strong woman."

Martha shook her head. "No, I'm not. I did what I had to do, that's all. It's all any of us can do."

She stood to carry her dishes to the sink, but Olivia placed a hand on her shoulder. "You sit and enjoy your coffee. I'll take care of the dishes."

An hour later, Martha's friend brought Brian home. Olivia studied the child while Martha and her friend talked. A handsome little boy with large brown eyes and longish dark hair that fell into his eyes, he had immediately climbed into his mother's lap and studied Olivia right back. It struck Olivia how much he resembled the pictures she had seen of her father yesterday when he was young. What would become of the boy? She knew firsthand how difficult it was to lose a parent as a small child. But at least she'd had her mother. Brian had nobody. A sense of heaviness settled in her chest as she contemplated the fate of the precious child before her. Did he know what was happening? Did he realize that his whole world was about to come crumbling down?

Martha's friend stood. "Well, I'd better be getting home. It was nice to meet you, Olivia."

Olivia forced a smile, although her heart throbbed with pain. "You, too."

After the woman left, Martha turned to her son. "Brian, this is a special person. Aunt Olivia."

The boy turned somber eyes to Olivia. "Aunt Owiv . . ." He blew out a breath and tried again.

"Aunt Owiv . . ." His brow furrowed in frustration.

"It's okay, Brian," said Olivia. "How about calling me Aunt 'O'?"

"Aunt O. Aunt O." He climbed down from his mother's lap and ventured closer. "Why you here, Aunt O?"

Olivia smiled. "I came to see you, Brian. And your mother."

"Me?"

"Yes, I wanted to meet you."

A big grin lit up the boy's face, and he crawled up next to her, wrapped his little arms around her neck, and kissed her cheek.

Olivia's eyes widened in astonishment. Martha laughed. "He likes you. Brian is very affectionate, as you can see."

The pain in Olivia's heart melted away as she returned the child's hug. The sweetness of his body pressed up against hers filled her with a warmth that spread through her entire being. Never having been around small children all that much, Olivia hadn't known quite what to expect. She certainly hadn't expected to feel an instant connection to a boy she'd never met. Still, it didn't mean she'd make a suitable mother substitute. Brian needed a stable, structured environment with a woman who knew how to address the needs of a child. This description definitely did not fit her, with her crazy schedule and haphazard eating habits. All she knew was horses, not children. She would pray hard for God to send just the right woman.

Chapter Thirteen

Olivia was glad to be home, despite the attachment she had developed to Martha and Brian. She promised to go back and visit in a couple of weeks, even though it would mean more time from work. Darcy would understand.

Her mind wandered back to Utah as she went about the routine of her day. No one was around when she finished her last trail ride, so she spent the next hour putting away the horses and tack. A weariness draped over her shoulders, and she looked forward to getting home, heating up a microwave dinner, and spending the evening watching mindless television so her over-stimulated brain could take a break.

As she left the barn, a male voice said, "Glad to see you're back."

Olivia jumped. Cam leaned against the barn door, an unreadable expression on his face, a piece of straw sticking out of one corner of his mouth.

"Gracious! You startled me."

"Sorry, I didn't mean to." He removed the straw, his eyes traveling over her face. "You look tired."

She laughed. "Seems like you always catch me at

my worst."

"I didn't mean it that way. I'm sure your trip was difficult."

His comment, no doubt meant to offer sympathy, stabbed at her heart. She'd tried to focus on other things during the day, but her thoughts kept circling back to Martha and Brian. She nodded and swallowed hard against the knot in her throat.

"Thank you for the phone call while I was gone. That was very thoughtful of you."

He tipped his head once. "Just wanted to let you know I was thinking about you."

Olivia peered at him, his expression still inscrutable. She didn't want to read too much into his kindness.

"So, you headed home?" he asked.

She lowered her eyes. "Yeah. As you pointed out, I not only *look* tired, I *am* tired."

They both continued to stand, neither making a move to walk to their vehicles. He cleared his throat and mumbled, "What about dinner?"

Her pulse quickened. Was he asking her out? Well, certainly not *out* like a date, of course. That would be . . . what, exactly? Improper? No, not really. Improbable? More likely. She couldn't trust her own emotions right now, so she tried not to overthink Cam's words.

"You don't have plans, do you?" he asked.

She shook her head. "I was just going to heat up something simple."

"I'm swinging by the diner. Why don't you join me? You have to eat, and it will save you from cooking. Even something simple."

The idea of not eating dinner alone suddenly sounded appealing. "Okay," she agreed, some of the weariness lifting from her shoulders.

He grinned. "Good, I'll follow you."

She nodded. "All right."

They walked in silence to their vehicles, Olivia shooting little glances at the man by her side whom she had known for a long time, yet hadn't paid much attention to. It seemed he had started going out of his way to be nice, and she wondered, yet again, if that's all there was to it. Her heart had taken two swift blows in a short time, and she had to be careful.

He waited for her to pull out, then fell in behind her. For some reason, the knowledge that Cam followed on the long, isolated road comforted her. She didn't know why, exactly. She'd never been nervous driving alone on the lonely road to and from the ranch. In the several minutes it took them to drive into town, her thoughts ricocheted around her brain, leaving her more confused than ever. But when she parked in the diner lot and he stopped his truck next to her car, hopping out quickly to open her door, all the confusion drained away, replaced by gratitude for his companionship.

She reminded herself not to make anything more out of this scenario than having dinner with a friend. Period. She might even enjoy his company if she stopped trying to analyze his intentions to death. They found a booth near the back of the diner. She slid into the red vinyl seat, tucked a stray strand of hair behind her ear, and stole a glance at the man sitting across from her before picking up the laminated menu that lay tucked behind the napkin holder. They spoke little as they perused their menus, both opting for hamburgers and fries. The smell of fresh coffee and grease from the fryers invoked a noisy reaction from her stomach, and she remembered she'd skipped lunch. She winced inwardly, hoping the general hubbub of the busy restaurant filled with chatter, laughter, and clanking of dishes camouflaged the sound. Cam either didn't notice or was too polite to comment.

Once the waitress had filled their water glasses and taken their order, she raised her eyes back to Cam's and offered him a shy smile. "Thank you. This was a good idea."

"My pleasure." He smiled back, and it struck her again what a sweet, honest face he had.

"So," they both said at the same time, then laughed.

"You first," she said.

His eyes locked on hers, and she saw genuine warmth and concern emanating from his soft brown eyes. "I just wanted to tell you again how sorry I am about your sister."

She drew in a sharp breath, and he continued, "I'm a good listener if you want to talk about it, but if you don't, it's fine. We can talk about something else or just enjoy a quiet dinner."

Olivia's eyes drifted to her hands in her lap. She hadn't had a chance to share her feelings with anyone, and the need to talk to somebody burned in her chest. She couldn't talk to her mother about Martha, as Mom still harbored hard feelings toward her resentful stepdaughter who'd made her early married years difficult. No doubt she would be sympathetic once she learned of Martha's illness, but she probably wouldn't be overly supportive. Darcy had been at work all day;

otherwise, Olivia might have shared some of her grief with her. Cam was a nice, understanding man who sat right across from her giving her an open invitation to unburden herself.

She crooked her index finger, swiped a tear from the corner of her eye, and, in a shaky voice, began the story of how she and her sister had remained estranged for so long, and now that she had found her, they didn't have much time. Cam let her talk, occasionally asking a question or inserting a comment. His eyes never left her face as she poured out her heart.

The waitress placed their meals before them just as Olivia finished. Sharing her pain with him had lightened her spirit, and she dug into her hamburger with a renewed appetite. The juice from the burger dribbled down her chin, and she wiped it away quickly, suddenly self-conscious about eating in front of Cam.

He chuckled and wiped his own chin. "Hard to keep clean eating the diner's burgers. But they're worth the mess."

She grinned. Cam was so unpretentious, unlike Kyle. Snippets of Kyle's arrogance replayed in her mind, and she wondered how she had failed to notice how pompous he had been. Perhaps, subconsciously, she had seen but chose to ignore the red flags that signaled they weren't right for each other. She'd been way too consumed with his good looks and the fact that a guy like him wanted to date her. She'd overlooked his character flaws.

"What are you thinking about?" he asked. "You look a million miles away."

Olivia refocused on the man in front of her. No way did she want to talk about Kyle. She hadn't even wanted her thoughts invaded by Kyle. They had just popped up out of nowhere. "Oh, nothing."

He raised an eyebrow but didn't respond.

Changing the subject, she said, "This is good. Much better than a frozen dinner."

"Most things are." He took another large bite of his burger and wiped the grease from his chin.

"True, but it's the one thing I can cook that usually doesn't end up a disaster."

His eyes twinkled. "Then you'd better marry a man who can cook."

"Great idea. Got any recommendations?" The minute the words flew off her tongue, she wanted to snatch them back. Heat infused her face at her flirtatiousness. She picked up her water and took a long sip to avoid looking at him.

He just chuckled. "I'll keep my eyes open."

She busied herself with chewing to keep her mouth from uttering any more foolishness. The rest of the meal passed in a somewhat awkward silence. When the waitress brought the bill, Cam reached for it. She laid a hand on his.

"Let me pay for my meal."

He snatched the check out from under her hand. "Nope. I asked you to dinner, remember?"

"Yes, but—"

"No 'buts.' I enjoyed your company." He rose and headed to the cash register.

She watched him thread his way through the tables and thought again how kind he was. She slowly made her way to his side as he finished paying the bill. Then he placed his hat on his head and his hand gently against her lower back to guide her out of the restaurant. As they stepped into the cool evening air, Olivia buttoned her jacket, feeling a subtle tension in the air between them. She glanced sideways at his face, illuminated by the soft glow of the parking lot lights. Once again, although an unreadable expression had settled into his features, a faint smile lifted the corners of his mouth. Their steps sounded unnaturally loud in the quietness of the deserted lot.

"Well," he said, as they reached her car. "Here we are. Thanks for joining me tonight."

"Thank you for asking." She opened her door, then turned and searched his face. He didn't seem in any hurry to leave.

He lowered his eyes, then said, hesitantly, "Look, Olivia, I . . ."

She waited. Was he going to tell her not to expect more from him than he was willing to give? Her impulsive comment about marriage candidates coupled with her impulsive kiss a few weeks ago had probably spooked him. He'd never expressed any interest in her, aside from colleagues who worked together. She needed to stop sending him signals of "desperate, man-hungry female."

He finally brought his eyes back to hers. "I enjoyed being with you tonight."

She didn't know if she was supposed to respond, but she replied, "I enjoyed it, too. Thanks for listening to me. I hope I didn't bore you to death."

A shy smile tugged at his lips. "Not at all. Look, I don't mean to be forward or presumptuous, and I don't know exactly where you stand after breaking up with your boyfriend and all, but . . ."

Her breath hitched. "Yes?"

"Well, I was wondering if you'd like to catch the movie that's playing this week at the cinema. I kind of wanted to see it, but it's no fun going by myself." His eyes immediately darted to the ground again. "But if I'm being too forward—"

Olivia felt her face stretch into a broad grin. "I'd love to go with you."

His head snapped up. "Yeah? Really? Oh, okay then. How about if I pick you up on Friday night and we can grab a bite to eat before the movie?"

She nodded. "Okay. Sounds good. But only if I can buy the popcorn."

He chuckled. "Deal. Well, I guess I'll see you at work tomorrow."

"See you tomorrow. Thanks again for tonight." She slid into her seat, and he closed the door behind her.

"Drive safe."

"You, too."

He waited until she had pulled out of her parking place, and she watched him in her rearview mirror until he disappeared from view. She hadn't even asked what movie was playing.

Chapter Fourteen

Well, so much for not being overly friendly. Cam had practically ambushed Olivia when she'd left the barn and, truth be told, he'd waited half an hour to do so. He did give himself points for not rushing to help her put away the riding equipment, as that seemed too contrived. Still, it might have been better than slinking around waiting for her to finish. But the subterfuge had panned out. She'd agreed to have dinner with him, and now they had an honest-to-goodness date. He should have checked to see what movie was playing this week, but the idea had simply popped up into his head and seemed like a golden opportunity. Not that he couldn't have broached the subject at work, but he never knew when or where they would run into each other at the ranch, and he didn't particularly want overhearing ears.

He liked the idea of getting to know Olivia better. The few women he'd dated in the past had, at least in the beginning, found the idea of dating a cowboy romantic. But the reality of maintaining a relationship with a man who worked long hours, made little money, and smelled like a barnyard more often than not, soon dampened the attraction. He'd sometimes wished for a woman like Ben and Ricky had—one who understood a man with ranching in his blood. But women like that were hard to find, and he had been content to keep the status quo with a simple, uncomplicated life. His singleness hadn't particularly bothered him until recently. How he had missed seeing the virtues in a woman like Olivia, he didn't know. Then again, she'd had a serious boyfriend until a few weeks ago, so he hadn't given her much thought. She had been off-limits, as far as he was concerned.

Cam hadn't particularly cared for Kyle on the few occasions he'd run into him at the ranch, and he didn't understand how Kyle failed to realize what a wonderful woman he'd discarded. Still, Kyle's loss was Cam's gain. Olivia had no illusions as to what a cowboy's job entailed, nor did she have any expectations that Cam would ever desire to do anything else, as did so many of the women he'd dated in the past. Olivia's whole life revolved around working with horses, so she understood the hard work, the risks involved, and what it took to get the job done.

She was also a sweet, wholesome, Christian woman. He didn't know when he'd stopped thinking of her as a kid. Perhaps at the wedding when he'd noticed how much of a woman she really was. It was also the first time he'd taken notice of her pretty girl-next-door appeal, with her long honey-blonde hair and cornflower blue eyes. If two people were well suited for each other, it was the two of them. And she'd been right there under his nose the whole time. Although he hadn't specifically prayed about it, perhaps God had placed the right woman directly in his path. He dismissed his earlier misgivings about their age difference. As adults, the seven-year difference hardly mattered, especially when they were as compatible as the two of them appeared to be. Friday night suddenly seemed a long way off.

~

It was probably a good thing he'd had to work on Friday. Cam found himself as nervous as a teenager, and the never-ending list of chores helped pass the time. He'd started the morning by helping Ricky deworm uncooperative, squirming calves and ended the late afternoon assisting Ben in pulling a calf from a heifer who was having difficulty delivering. As the long day ended, he looked and smelled rode hard and put away wet. He would have collapsed into a worn-out heap if it weren't for the adrenaline pumping through his veins at the anticipation of his date with Olivia.

He led his horse back to the barn, happy to see Olivia finishing her riding lesson. He tipped his hat at the student exiting the paddock and ran a hand through his sweat-soaked hair. Olivia's face lit up when she saw him approach.

"Whoa, cowboy, you look done in. Are you still up for tonight?" Her eyes teased him. They'd exchanged a few flirty moments at the ranch since their dinner a few nights before.

"I'll get a second wind after I've had a shower."

She laughed. "I hope so. The first wind you're carrying around doesn't smell so great."

He feigned offense. "Is that so? Well, if I weren't a gentleman, I would say the same about you."

She smacked his arm playfully. "I don't stink. I smell like a horse. A delightful aroma."

"If you say so."

"Don't worry, I'll shower before you pick me up."

"Thank you. I'd like us to be acceptable in public." He winked at her. "See you at seven?"

"Perfect. I'll be ready."

~

Olivia had, most delightfully, cleaned up nicely. She wore a full, calf-length, white skirt, a flowery red blouse, and flat white sandals. It was only the second time Cam had ever seen her in something other than jeans and boots, and he liked what he saw. She had washed her long hair, which hung loose and gave off the pleasant scent of something flowery rather than horse. The last rays of the waning sun danced on the individual strands of her hair, setting them ablaze in gold.

Cam wore khakis and a dark blue button-down shirt, hoping to appear smart, yet casual. His shirt fit snugly against his muscled frame.

"You look beautiful," he said, unable to take his eyes off her.

"You don't look so bad yourself," she answered, giving him an appreciative once-over.

He held out his arm. "Shall we?"

Before heading to the movies, they ate at a popular Mexican restaurant on the main thoroughfare. After dinner, they strolled the couple of blocks to the cinema, enjoying the rare warm evening and an unrushed agenda.

They stopped before the entrance to the theatre and Cam studied the advertised featured attraction next to the box office. His heart gave a lurch, and he turned to Olivia, feeling the egg running down his face.

Olivia looked from the marquee to him. "You

really wanted to see 'The Troll From Outer Space?'"

He felt his face growing warm. "Well, to be perfectly honest, I didn't actually know what was playing. I just used the movie as an excuse to ask you out."

She laughed. "Thank goodness. Otherwise, I'd have to question your taste in movies."

"If you'd just as soon skip the film, it's okay with me."

"I don't know. I'd hate to deprive you of this once-in-a-lifetime opportunity. But, in all honesty, I'd prefer to pass if you really don't mind."

He shot her an apologetic grin. "Is this your way of getting out of buying the popcorn?"

She rolled her eyes. "Cowboy, if I don't have to watch this excellent example of cinematography, I'll make you all the popcorn you want back at my place."

"You drive a hard bargain. I had my heart set on this film."

She laughed again. "I'll see if I can find us something to watch in my DVD collection."

"As you wish."

They drove back to her apartment, chuckling over the movie they'd decided against, and Cam's bumbling attempt to ask her out by pretending he wanted someone to see it with him. She unlocked her door and tossed her keys and purse onto a side table. Cam's eyes took in her small, mismatched living room.

"It's Early American garage sale," she said, as she watched him looking around. "But it's comfortable and it's paid for."

"It looks quite cozy. My apartment should look so good."

"The DVDs are in here," she said, pointing him to a small cabinet. "Your choice, since you didn't get to see 'The Troll From Outer Space.' I'll go make popcorn." She disappeared into a room to the left, which he presumed was the kitchen.

He settled on an Indiana Jones movie and had it ready to go by the time she returned bearing a large bowl of microwave popcorn and two water bottles. They sat on an ancient, sagging sofa, their feet propped on the coffee table in front of them.

Halfway through the movie, the long day hit him hard, and he couldn't hold his eyes open. He laid his head back to rest his eyes for just a moment, and the next thing he knew, he awoke to find Olivia's head on his chest, her soft hair spilling over his arm, and the movie credits rolling. Although he could have happily remained just like they were, it wouldn't be proper for him to be seen leaving her apartment in the wee hours of the morning. He gently wiggled out from under her weight, laid her head against a couch pillow, and lifted her legs to the sofa. Looking around, he spied an afghan folded up on a rocking chair. He covered her with the afghan, bent and kissed her temple, and then let himself out.

Chapter Fifteen

"We've got to stop falling asleep in each other's company," Olivia said the next day at the ranch. She had driven up as Cam got out of his truck, and they walked to the barn together, their boots crunching along the graveled pathway.

He smiled down at her."Sorry, I guess I'm just a boring guy. Maybe next time we should try sky-diving. It's hard to sleep when jumping from an airplane."

Her eyes widened. "No thanks. Boring is fine. Excitement is overrated."

Darcy emerged from the tack room carrying a saddle. "Hey, you two. How was the movie?"

Olivia and Cam exchanged glances. "It was great," said Olivia. "I highly recommend you and Ben see 'The Troll From Outer Space.'"

Frown lines appeared between Darcy's eyes, and she looked from one to the other. "Am I to assume you're joking?"

They continued to the tack room chuckling, leaving Darcy shaking her head.

"We really should have enlightened her," Olivia said, removing a harness from a peg on the wall.

"Nah, let her wonder." Cam grabbed a set of reins and draped them over his arm. "By the way, it's nice to see you back to your usual grubby self."

Olivia flattened her lips. "If you think I'm leading trail rides in a skirt, you're sadly mistaken."

He nodded. "It was just a thought. Might have drummed up more business."

"Yeah, well, I don't see you making your rounds in khakis and loafers."

"That's because I don't want to break my neck. Besides, nobody around here cares how I look."

"Or how you smell."

His eyebrows shot up in mock indignation. "That was a low blow. If I don't reek of sweat and cows by the end of the day, I haven't been earning my paycheck."

She glanced around quickly, then closed the small gap between them, laying her head against his chest and inhaling deeply. "Mmm. Let me breathe in your intoxicating aroma of soap and water before you get to work."

He laughed and cupped his hand around the back of her head, holding her against him. "Breathe away." Resting his chin on the top of her head, he added, "And I will memorize the fragrance of your shampoo before your hair smells of horse."

It felt so good snuggled up against Cam's strong chest. How she wished they could stay like this. All too soon, he let her go and took a step back.

"So, do you want to try going out next weekend when we both have the day off?" he asked. "Maybe we can take a nap in the afternoon and stay awake for a whole evening."

Her smile slipped from her face. "I would love to, but I promised Martha I would visit her. I don't know how much longer I'll have her in my life."

He nodded. "I understand. We'll plan something for when you get back. Gotta get to work. Have a good day." He finished gathering his equipment, blew her a kiss, and headed for the horse stalls.

"You, too," she called after him. Conflicting emotions churned through Olivia's mind. Her heart felt light and giddy at her unfolding relationship with Cam, while at the same time, it sat like a heavy rock in her chest at the thought of losing Martha. She wanted to spend as much time with Martha as possible, but she knew she would miss Cam while she was gone. Surprised at how quickly she was falling for him, she tried to rein in her feelings. She knew she needed to proceed cautiously. Although Cam seemed perfect on the surface—the kind of man she'd dreamed of all her life—she still didn't know him all that well. Rushing headlong into a relationship had not worked out well with Kyle, and she had no wish to repeat her mistake. But her foolish heart betrayed her by skittering every time Cam was around.

~

"Aunt O, look at me!" Brian called from the top of the slide before he slid to the bottom.

Olivia smiled and clapped her hands. "Good job, Brian." She had taken her nephew to the park while Martha was at a doctor's appointment. Olivia loved watching the energetic little boy run and play, completely innocent and carefree. He had taken to her from the first time she'd met him, and his unconditional childish affection stirred her heart in ways she'd never known existed. After only a couple of visits, she found herself becoming attached to him, as well. The first time he'd wrapped his chubby little arms around her neck, she'd felt an instant connection. She wanted to shower him with love and protect him from the hurt she knew was coming.

She watched as he joined in a game with a couple of other children, their laughter filling the crisp air as they chased each other from one end of the park to the other. A young woman plopped down on the bench beside her.

"Which one is yours?" she asked.

Olivia pointed toward the child who was little more than a blur. "The one in the striped shirt. He's my nephew, Brian."

"I've seen him here before. With a lady who looks like she has cancer. At least her head is always wrapped in a scarf."

Olivia nodded. "That's my sister, Martha. She has terminal breast cancer."

The woman made a sympathetic clucking with her tongue. "I'm so sorry. That will be hard on the poor child." A sweet smile formed on her face. "But he's certainly blessed to have you."

A tight band formed around Olivia's chest. She didn't want to contradict the woman's errant conclusion that Olivia would be a fixture in Brian's life, helping to fill the void after his mother was gone. Not trusting herself to speak, she swallowed against the thickness in her throat. How she wished circumstances could be different. But she couldn't adequately care for a young child. It wouldn't be fair to him. Surely there was someone more suited among Martha's friends and acquaintances. He would be much better off with a family, even if they weren't blood relatives. Martha hadn't brought the subject up again, so Olivia assumed she had the situation covered. But she didn't want to pry. She knew talking about Brian's future would be painful for Martha.

"Aunt O, did you see me? Did you see how fast I can run?" Brian suddenly appeared at her side, his face flushed, and out of breath. His dark eyes shone with pride.

Olivia forced a smile. "Yes, I did, Brian. You are very fast."

"Watch me again." He took off like a bolt of lightning streaking across the sky.

The woman next to Olivia chuckled. "Oh to have their energy. Mine is the little girl hanging upside down from the monkey bars."

Olivia's gaze was drawn to a child with two long pigtails dangling in the air, her shirt raised up to expose her belly.

"I used to worry that she'd fall on her head, but I've given up. Mallory is such a little tomboy." As if to prove her mother's point, the little girl righted herself and quickly climbed down the monkey bars, joining in the chase game with Brian and the others.

Olivia couldn't imagine having the responsibility of keeping a child safe, especially a rambunctious one like Mallory, and a new admiration for parents of young children filled her awareness. Children had to be watched every second. It just reinforced her stance that she would not make a good mother. Still, she savored the precious time she spent with Brian.

She chatted with the young mother for another

few minutes as the children continued to burn off energy. Then, glancing at her watch, she called, "Brian, it's time to go. Your mother should be home by now."

Without complaint, the child stopped his play and returned to where she sat. "Can we have peanut butter and jelly sandwiches for lunch?"

She brushed the sweaty hair from his eyes. "If that's what you'd like."

"It's my favorite."

"It used to be my favorite, too." Olivia turned to the woman. "It was nice meeting you. I hope to see you again sometime." She didn't know if their paths would cross again, and she hadn't told the woman that she didn't live here. She hadn't wanted the discussion to turn to what would become of Brian. Her conscience couldn't take any more guilt. She was doing a good enough job of piling the guilt on all by herself.

They walked the two blocks back to Martha's house. Or rather, she walked while Brian danced backward, skipped, and ran in circles around her. She was glad to see Martha's car in the driveway. Brian raced through the back door, banging the screen behind him, calling, "Mommy, guess what?"

Olivia didn't hear the details of the conversation, other than Brian's excited childish voice relaying something of significance that had occurred at the playground. Martha turned from her animated son and smiled at her when she stepped into the kitchen.

"It sounds like you two had a good time."

Olivia nodded. "Yes. I think Brian should be sufficiently worn out to take a nice, long nap."

"No, Aunt O. I'm not tired."

Brian continued to bounce around the room while

Olivia prepared sandwiches. After lunch, he crashed, barely missing laying his cheek in his plate. Olivia carried him to his room and laid him on his bed, laying a thin blanket over him. She paused for a moment in the doorway, relishing the sweetness of the sleeping child, and her heart stirred with love.

Returning to the kitchen, she found Martha washing the few lunch dishes. "Let me do that," she said, removing the dishrag from Martha's hand. "Sit down. You look exhausted. How did your doctor's appointment go?"

They had refrained from discussing the appointment until Brian was asleep. Martha returned to the table and took a long drink from her iced tea. "It went fine, other than sitting around the doctor's office all morning drains me. Right now I'm stable. He's starting me on a new supplement to help alleviate the fatigue."

Olivia finished rinsing the plates and set them in the dish rack. Joining Martha at the table, she said, "I wish I lived closer so I could be here to help you."

Martha reached over and squeezed her hand. "I'm just grateful that you can come as often as you do. I know it takes you away from your work and things you need to be doing at home."

"I don't mind. My bosses are very understanding."

"What about the young man in your life?" Martha's eyes twinkled with mischief.

Olivia's jaw dropped. "What? How—"

"Oh, come on. You've thrown his name around more than once. Tell me about him."

Heat crept up Olivia's neck into her face. "Is it

that obvious?"

Martha grinned. "I've got cancer but I'm not blind."

Olivia grinned. "I guess I don't hide my emotions very well." She'd already filled Martha in on her two-year relationship with Kyle and how he'd dumped her, but she hadn't talked much about Cam. At least, she didn't think she had. The last time she'd visited, she and Cam hadn't done much more than tiptoe around their blossoming feelings for each other. Martha had obviously heard otherwise.

"You've got that 'glow' about you. Like a woman in love."

Olivia shook her head. "Oh, no. It's way too early to use the 'L' word. We're barely getting to know each other." She searched for the right words. "But, Martha, Cam is such a nice man. Thoughtful and sweet—a total gentleman. And a Christian."

"That's important." Martha's smile faded. "I think, maybe, that's why none of my relationships worked out. I was looking for love in all the wrong places." She fiddled with the napkin holder, removing a napkin and wiping her nose before the smile returned to her face.

"And we're so compatible," Olivia went on. "We both love working at the ranch, and he has a wonderful sense of humor, and we like all the same things."

"Where's he from originally? What's his background?"

The question stumped Olivia, and she had to admit she didn't know. They'd never talked about his family, where he grew up, or how he ended up at Whispering Winds Ranch. Her brows furrowed in thought. She'd told him everything about her background, but he'd not said anything about his.

"To be honest, I don't know. We haven't talked much about his past."

Martha leveled her gaze at her sister. "Honey, take some advice from an older woman with some miles on her. Before you get too deeply invested in this relationship, you need to know where he's been. You don't want any surprises down the road."

Chapter Sixteen

"Cam, tell me about your past—where you grew up, about your family, everything." They sat across the table from each other at the local pizza parlor, having decided to try to get through an entire evening without falling asleep.

Cam's head jerked back in surprise. "Whoa. Where did all this come from?"

Olivia persisted. "I've told you everything about me. But I don't know anything about you."

He chuckled and shook his head. "Well, there's not much to tell. My history is pretty boring, like the rest of my life."

"I still want to hear about it."

Cam took a bite of pizza, swallowed, and washed it down with a gulp of water. "Do you mind if I talk and eat at the same time? I'm starving."

She grinned. "Of course. As long as you don't talk with your mouth full."

He took another bite and spoke around the food. "No deal. I'm hungry."

"Cam—"

He wiped his mouth. "Fine. I grew up in a small

town in northern Wyoming called Westerville. My dad works at a chemical plant and my mother is a stay-at-home mom. My uncle owns a cattle ranch not too far from town where I spent a lot of time, and where I developed my love of ranching. I graduated in the middle one-third of my class at Westerville High School. Again, disgustingly average. Never went to college. I worked for my uncle for a few years, then came here. End of story." Except for a couple of details like *why* he came here.

"Does your family still live there?"

"Yes. I go up and visit from time to time."

"Do you have any brothers or sisters?"

Drat. He didn't want to talk about Annette. "One sister, younger. Annette."

Olivia pursed her lips. "Cam, you're making this like pulling teeth. What does Annette do? Is she married? Does she have kids?"

Cam sighed. "She works as a receptionist in a doctor's office. Divorced. One son, Finn. We're not close."

"That's it?"

"That's it."

She eyed him warily, obviously wondering what he'd left out.

"Do you want to put me through any more inquisition, or can I eat now?"

She obviously did, but she dropped her eyes. "No, I guess not."

"Good. I told you my history was boring." He bit off another piece of pizza and tried to smile with his mouth full. A little prickle of guilt jabbed at his conscience for not telling her the rest of the story. But he didn't share that episode with anyone. What would they think of him?

~

Talking about his family with Olivia had ripped a scab off a never-healing wound. After he returned to his apartment, a strong urge to connect with them pulled at him. Reaching for the phone, he called his parents.

"Cam, what a nice surprise." Just hearing his mother's voice immediately warmed him. "What's going on?"

"Nothing, Mom. Can't I call just to talk?"

"Of course, dear. Let me get your father." Without holding her hand over the mouthpiece, she yelled, "Jim, pick up the extension. It's Cam."

Cam flinched, yanked the phone away from his ear, and grinned.

"Son? How are you?" His father's voice boomed through the receiver. For some reason, his father always talked loudly on the phone, perhaps as a long-ingrained habit from when phone connections were not always the best in their remote part of the country.

Still holding the phone a few inches from his ear, he answered, "Fine, Dad. What's new with you?"

"Oh, nothing much. I'm thinking of retiring next year when I turn sixty-five."

"Good for you. What will you do with all your spare time?" Cam settled against his headboard and propped a pillow behind his head.

"Drive me crazy, that's what," said his mother. "I can't imagine having your father underfoot all day."

"Maybe you need to get a job, Mom. Get out of the house."

She huffed. "I just might. So, what have you been

doing?"

"Same old, same old. You know, mucking out stalls, wrangling cattle." He paused, debating whether or not to share Olivia with them. He'd never talked much about other women he'd dated, but for some reason, he felt compelled to tell them about her. "I'm dating a very nice lady. Her name's Olivia. She works at the ranch leading trail rides and giving riding lessons."

"Oh!" His mother's shriek caused him to punch the speaker button and lay the phone on his bedside table, far away from his ringing ear. "How wonderful! When do we get to meet her?"

He chuckled. "Hold on. We're not quite to 'meet the parents' level yet."

His father's laughter filled the space between them. "You know your mother. Next thing you know, she'll be ordering wedding invitations."

"I would hold off on that for now, Mom. At least until you know her last name so you can print it correctly on the invitations."

"So, are things serious?" his mother prodded.

Cam hesitated, searching for the right answer. Things were not *yet* serious, but he couldn't deny the fact he wouldn't mind moving in that direction. He couldn't imagine a more perfect woman. "We're just getting to know each other. But the potential is there to develop into something more."

His mother whooped. "I always knew God had someone special out there for you."

He grinned. Good old Mom. "Well, if and when we get to the 'someone special' point, I'll let you know. You'd like her, though. She's a lot like Ann . . ." He closed his eyes. He hadn't meant to bring up Annette, but the fact was Olivia did remind him a lot of his sister. At least before. He swallowed, then asked softly, "How is Annette?"

"She's fine. She's dating a nice man. And Finn is growing like a weed." The tension in his mother's tone was unmistakable.

Cam nodded, but his parents obviously couldn't see. "Good, that's good. Tell her I said hi."

His father cleared his throat. "Why don't you give her a call? She'd love to hear from you."

Cam sighed. "I'm not sure she would. She's never completely forgiven me."

"Son, what happened was an accident. It could have happened to anyone," said his father.

"But it didn't. It happened to me and Finn."

"But everything turned out all right," argued his mother. "I hate seeing you and your sister still so distant with one another."

"So do I, Mom. Look, I need to go. I'll look at coming up in a few weeks."

"Will you bring Olivia?" His mom's voice bounced back to cheerful with a hint of hope.

"I'm not sure yet." He explained how Olivia was having to take a lot of time off to be with her sister. His parents expressed their sympathy and understanding.

"Well, whenever you're able, we'd love to meet her," said his father.

"You could always come south," said Cam.

"We'll try, but it's hard to get away what with your father's job and me taking care of Finn after school."

"Yeah, I know." Cam ran a hand through his hair.

"Anyway, I need to go," he repeated. "It was good to talk to you."

"You, too. We love you," said his mother.

"Love you both, too. Bye."

He disconnected the call and sat pondering his family. At some point, if his relationship moved forward with Olivia, he would have to tell her about what happened, especially if he took her to Westerville. But not now. Not when everything was so new and promising.

The thought of Olivia brought a smile to his face. He looked forward to going to work each day hoping to run into her and trying to make sure he did. The euphoria that had consumed him these past few weeks constituted a completely new experience for him. He'd never had this unbridled happiness with anyone else. The anticipation of being with her brought on the visceral sensation of "butterflies in the stomach," something he'd never understood before now. As much as he'd shaken his head over Ben and Ricky falling in love, he realized he had become "one of them" now, and he rather liked it.

He looked at his watch. He'd just dropped her off an hour ago. Would he seem too much like a junior high student if he called her before going to bed?

"Show some restraint, man," he groused aloud. "At least pretend to play hard to get."

His phone chirped, startling him. Glancing at the caller ID, he chuckled. "Hi, did you miss me already?"

The smile slid from his face at her words. Martha had died suddenly.

Chapter Seventeen

Cam stood by the graveside holding tightly to Olivia's hand. Her other hand gripped a soggy tissue that she periodically swiped under her eyes. She had said very little on the drive to Utah, nor during the service, which a group of ladies from Martha's church had organized. Olivia had been grateful for their help, not knowing who to contact or how to go about taking care of all the details surrounding a loved one's death.

Martha's will had designated her pastor as the executor of her will—a job Olivia was thankful not to have to do. Martha's rental house had been furnished, so aside from some personal belongings, there wasn't much to clean out. The church ladies assured Olivia they would take care of that task. Martha's money had been left in a trust for Brian, who was staying with a neighbor for the time being. Olivia wasn't sure if she imagined it or not, but it seemed like Cam had acted strangely when he met Brian. Perhaps he didn't like children, and that thought saddened her. Or he might have simply been surprised to find out about Brian. Olivia realized she hadn't told Cam about him, mostly because talking about Brian filled her with guilt, and she didn't want another person trying to talk her into taking the child.

But right now, her feelings were so scattered that she couldn't make any sense of them, so she didn't try to examine them too closely.

"I didn't expect her to go so soon," she whispered, yet again, the wet tissue doing little to stem the steady stream of tears. "I mean, I knew it was coming, but the last time I saw her, she looked so good."

Cam put his arm around her and pulled her to his side. Her mother, who had chided Olivia for not letting her know of Martha's condition, stood on her other side, grim-faced. It was bad enough losing Martha, but her mother's anger at not being informed twisted Olivia's insides.

"I meant to tell you," Olivia had said, "but I didn't know how you would react to my reconnecting with Martha. Then before I got the chance, she died."

"It was still wrong not to let me know right away," said her mother. "Martha and I might have had our differences, but we were still family."

Olivia had held her tongue about all the things her mother had said in the past about Martha. Now she dealt not only with her grief over losing Martha, but the fact she hadn't even given her mother a chance to mend fences with her stepdaughter before she died. Not to mention her heartache for Brian, who seemed a little bewildered by everything. Thank goodness for Cam. He'd stood beside her, offering quiet support as Olivia sleepwalked through the whole ordeal. The only good to come out of the nightmarish past few days was the instant bond her mother formed with Cam.

"He's a good man, Olivia," she'd said, "hang on

to him."

Olivia's heart had swelled with her mother's approval. Although she'd never said anything against Kyle, her mother hadn't been particularly demonstrative with her affection toward him, either.

Cam nudged her forward to toss her rose into the grave. She stood looking down at the coffin, feeling robbed of the time she could have had Martha in her life, but glad she'd had her at the end, no matter how short the time. She kissed the white rose in her hand and dropped it onto the coffin. "Goodbye, sweet sister. We'll meet again one day."

Cam gently led her back to where the pastor stood, as a small group of people filed past to offer their condolences. She didn't know any of them, but the fact they had known and loved her sister was comforting.

A short, gray-haired lady stopped and touched Olivia's arm. "We've arranged a luncheon back at the church for the family."

Family. All two of them. Brian had been whisked away by the neighbor after the funeral at the church, not attending the graveside service. The neighbor had explained that everything was too confusing for him right now.

"Thank you." Although the last thing Olivia felt like doing was eating, it had been kind of the church to do so much.

They made their way slowly across the uneven, grassy expanse of the cemetery to where Cam's truck waited, the bright sunshine and colorful flowers placed on grave sites incongruous to the coldness wrapping itself around Olivia's body. Cam opened the front passenger door, directing Olivia's mother to ride up front, then opened the back door for her. Olivia stared, unseeing, out the window as they drove back to the church. She just had to get through the next hour, then they could be on their way.

The delicious aroma of warm food filled the fellowship hall, and despite the dull ache in her belly, Olivia knew she needed to eat. She'd had nothing this morning except for a cup of coffee, which had only soured her stomach. Two ladies on the kitchen staff directed them to go through the serving line, and Olivia did her best to take a small sample of everything.

As she forced down the lovingly prepared food, several more people came by the table to express their sympathy. Just before they finished, a woman pressed a small ornamental box into her hand.

"It's Martha's jewelry. I don't think there's anything much of value in there, but I thought you might like to have it."

Olivia squeezed her hands around the box, willing the tears not to start again. "Thank you so much. For everything." The jewelry and the stack of photo albums were the only things she'd taken from Martha's house. She would keep the albums for Brian until he was older.

The woman hugged her. "We only knew Martha for a short time, but we loved her."

Me, too. Olivia smiled through the tears that stung her eyes, despite her resolve not to cry again.

They finally made their last goodbyes, then stopped at the neighbor's house to see Brian one more time before leaving.

"Aunt O!" he cried when he saw them at the door. He ran to her throwing his arms around her waist.

She knelt and pulled the little body into her arms, inhaling deeply of his sweet childish smell. She held him for a long moment before rocking back on her heels and gazing into his serious brown eyes. Brushing the hair from his forehead, she said, "I'll come visit you as often as I can, Brian. I promise."

He clung to her again before the neighbor gently pried him away. "Brian, there are some cookies in the kitchen for you. Why don't you go get them?"

Brian hesitated, looking between the lady and Olivia, then did as he was told. When he had left the room, the woman pulled Olivia onto the porch. Cam and her mother followed.

"Look, I don't mean to upset you, but I think it would be better if you didn't visit Brian for a while."

"What? Why?" The knife twisted deeper into Olivia's heart.

The woman sighed. "There is a couple from the church who wants to adopt Brian. We all think it would be less confusing if he is given time to bond with them and move on. You coming in and out of his life will only disrupt that process."

Olivia's bottom lip began to quiver, and she quickly bit down on it to stop from breaking down again. She drew shaky breaths, taking in the woman's words and reasons, but not wanting to hear them. Finally, unable to trust her voice, she nodded. She allowed Cam and her mother to guide her back to the truck, the tears flowing in an endless stream. As Cam started to open her door, she put out her hand, stepped back to the porch, and said, "Please tell him goodbye and that I love him."

Returning to the truck, she allowed the deep,

racking sobs to overtake her. Would Brian think she'd abandoned him? She hadn't counted on not maintaining contact with him. Why had God allowed her to find her sister and nephew only to snatch them away?

The long, quiet ride home seemed interminable. Once they had dropped Olivia's mother off at her house, Cam turned the truck away from Olivia's apartment.

"Where are we going?" Olivia twisted in her seat looking behind her, then at Cam.

"To the ranch. I think I know what you need right now. Some horse therapy."

She closed her eyes, acknowledging the truth in his words. Even though the sun was quickly disappearing in a blaze of oranges and reds into the horizon, an evening ride would soothe her soul like nothing else in the world could.

They pulled up beside the house and walked to the paddock. Olivia was surprised to see Darcy waiting with Maggie and Kimber saddled up and ready to go. Darcy gave her a brief hug without speaking, then headed back to the house.

The horses started off at a leisurely pace, Olivia and Cam riding in companionable silence. With no particular destination in mind, they ended up at the small brook, a comforting place to let the stress of life melt away. They dismounted, removed their shoes and socks, and settled on the edge, letting the cold water flow over their feet. The rhythmic movement of the water over the rocks created a calming, almost mesmerizing effect on her mood, as though her worries washed downstream with the current. The pungent odor of wet moss and grass filled her with peace and the simple joy of being alive. Dusk enveloped them in its gray cloak, but there was no need to hurry. The horses could find their way back in the dark blindfolded.

"Thank you, Cam. I needed this." She leaned against him, resting her head on his shoulder.

"I know," he murmured against her hair.

They sat without talking until an almost full moon rose high in the sky and stars appeared in the inky blackness. She tipped her head back to gaze at the stars."The sky is so beautiful."

He glanced upward, then back down at her. "Not as beautiful as you."

Her breath caught. Cam had never said anything so personal to her before. She brought her eyes to his face, reflected in the soft glow of the moonlight. Slowly, he lowered his head and brushed her lips with his. Tingles of heat spread through her body like a fiery current, and she wrapped her arms around his neck to pull him closer. Her heart pounded at the sensation of his warm mouth on hers. Everything else around them faded away—the sound of the brook, the chill of the evening air, even the sadness of the last few days. All too soon, he drew back, tucking her head against him again.

"I've wanted to do that for a long time," he murmured.

She raised up and looked at him. "Yeah?"

"Yeah."

"So why didn't you?"

"I was waiting for the right time."

"And?"

"And what?"

"Did the kiss live up to your expectations?" Her

voice held a hint of tease.

He pondered a moment. "I'm not sure. I'd better check again." He cupped the back of her head and drew her to him, kissing her with more firmness than before. Then he pulled away, licked his lips, and said, "I would say it exceeded my expectations. You're an amazing woman, Olivia."

"And you're an amazing man." She nestled against him, feeling as though she could handle anything with this man by her side. His strong, steady presence reassured her that everything would be okay.

A cool breeze stirred the night air, and Olivia shivered.

"You're cold. And it's late. We'd better be heading back before people start wondering what happened to us."

As loathe as she was for the magical evening to end, she disentangled herself from Cam's arms and reached for her shoes and socks. How a day that had started out so awful had turned out to be so wonderful, she couldn't imagine. She only knew Cam was responsible and for that, she felt herself falling for him even harder. He was so in tune with her feelings, knowing without asking how to make her feel better. She'd heard the term "soul mates" before but had always dismissed it as something not attainable in the real world. Now she was rethinking her former opinion. She'd never had such a connection with anyone, someone who knew her so instinctively. She loved the fact that Cam was so grounded, not letting anything upset him, and she loved his simple, uncomplicated lifestyle.

The horses picked up their pace as they neared the

barn, obviously ready to get to their dinner. Cam and Olivia untacked the horses quickly and put them into their stalls. Then he slung an arm around her and led her to his truck.

They rode back to her apartment in silence, as Olivia relived the past couple of hours. Cam's kiss and his declaration of admiration for her filled her with unspeakable joy, and part of her wanted to move the budding relationship along faster. But another part of her cautioned her to slow down and appreciate every special moment. She stole little sideways glances at him as they drove the lonely road back into town. His features, which had once seemed so plain and nondescript, now stirred her with an unmistakable longing. He caught her looking a couple of times and gave her a sweet smile, which caused her heart to swell with an emotion she was reluctant to acknowledge as love. Still, whether she acknowledged it or not, she knew she was falling hard for him. Something clicked in her mind warning her not to be too happy because the good times never lasted, but she shoved the thought away. Nothing was going to spoil this special time.

Chapter Eighteen

"How's Olivia doing?" asked Ben the next morning as they readied their horses to ride out to the pastures.

"She'll be okay," replied Cam. "Her sister's death was hard on her, but not unexpected. She's taking a couple of days off to rest, then she'll be back in the saddle, so to speak."

"You've been good for her." Ben placed his left foot in the stirrup and swung up onto Malachi's back.

Cam followed suit on Windsong. "She's been good for me."

The horses walked side by side, not in any hurry to climb the steep hill to the upper pastures. "So," Ben said, "does this mean things are getting serious between you two?"

Cam took a deep breath and thought for a moment. "I don't know. I've always admired Olivia, you know that. And since we've gotten closer, I've seen other sides to her that I like a lot." He took off his hat and pushed back a lock of hair that hung down in his eyes. "But I don't want to rush into anything."

Ben laughed. "You'd better snatch her up before

some other guy comes along. Don't wait too long."

Cam snorted. "Don't be marrying us off yet. We're just getting to know each other."

"Okay, but don't say I didn't warn you."

Cam didn't worry too much about Ben's warning. From the signals Olivia was putting out, it was clear how she felt about him. He wasn't completely blind. And he had to admit his heart was moving faster than his head. But although the relationship had blossomed into something potentially meaningful, part of him still held back. He wanted to proceed carefully, knowing that he couldn't let his emotions overrule his good judgment. It took time to nurture a relationship and build trust. He needed to be patient. And he needed to be sure beyond a shadow of a doubt before taking things further. Still, getting to know Olivia better was a welcome thought.

~

"How about going hiking with me tomorrow?" Cam didn't even pretend to linger after work anymore hoping to run into Olivia after she finished her riding lessons or trail rides. He simply hung out in plain sight, shooting her encouraging grins while she interacted with her clients. He loved watching her teach both children and adults with her usual patience and competence. Her love for her work shone in everything she did.

"Sounds good. Where and when?" She hefted a saddle from Dandy's back. Cam stepped in and took it from her arms.

"There's a park with a trailhead marked just outside of town. I've always meant to explore it, but never got around to it."

She shot him a mischievous grin. "Is this like the troll movie you wanted to see?"

"You're never going to let me forget that, are you?"

"Probably not." She gathered the rest of the tack and headed toward the barn.

"Fine. I can't wait to get something on you to hold over your head." He trailed after her.

"Ha! Good luck with that." She went into the tack room and wiped down the reins and halter before hanging them up. "I'm a pretty tough nut to crack."

He slung the saddle onto the rack. "Oh, I will. Just you wait." He stepped toward her and pulled her into his arms, planting a soft kiss on her lips.

She sighed and leaned into him. "When you do that, all my defenses come crashing down."

"Good," he whispered, his mouth just inches from hers. "I want you defenseless."

"That's not fair." But she didn't seem terribly perturbed as she raised her lips to his again.

~

The next day dawned clear and sunny, with wispy white clouds floating in a vast expanse of brilliant blue sky. Cam picked her up early, and they swung by the market to buy some bread, cheese, and fruit for a picnic lunch. Olivia rolled down the truck window to let the warm summer breeze flow through the cab, bringing with it the smell of freshly cut grass and wildflowers. Her hair, pulled back in its usual ponytail, fluttered in the wind, the rays of the sun streaking it with a radiant gold. Cam thought he'd never seen a more beautiful sight. Imagine. Pretty, vivacious Olivia actually falling for a plain, simple man like him. He couldn't explain it, but it sure felt good.

They parked at the entrance to the trailhead and hopped out, carrying their lunch and water bottles in their backpacks.

"I've never been here," Olivia said, "even though it's so close."

"Good. We'll explore it together."

"The sign at the entrance says it's a two-mile hike to an overlook."

"Sounds good. Are you up for a long walk?" He looked down at her.

"I am if you are."

Cam took her hand, and they headed into the wooded area made up of ponderosa pines interspersed with hardwoods. Their feet crunched along the dead leaves, pine needles, and branches littering the trail floor as they ventured deeper into the shaded canopy that blocked the warm beams of the sun. The temperature drop brought a chill to the air, raising goosebumps on Olivia's arms. Cam stopped and helped her put on her jacket. The only sounds in the largely deserted forest were their footsteps and the insistent call of two happy birds serenading each other.

The trail wound steadily uphill for several hundred feet before leveling out in a grassy knoll, where the sunlight filtered through the sparser trees. All too soon, the trail picked up again, heading back into the woods with a vertical climb. Olivia dug her boots into the spongy forest floor, grabbing hold of saplings and roots to pull herself upward. A recent rain had made the terrain slightly slippery, so she picked her way carefully.

"Now I know why I've never hiked this trail

before," Olivia puffed. She paused at a leveled-out area to catch her breath.

"Come on, wimp," Cam teased. "You can't be that out of shape."

She narrowed her eyes at him. "I'm probably in better shape than you are, old man."

"Ouch! That remark hurt."

"So did calling me a wimp."

He laughed. "Let's call a truce and take a water break before pressing on."

"It's a deal." Olivia sank onto a mostly flat, mossy rock that was partially exposed to the sun and reached for her water bottle. After a long drink, she said, "At least it will be downhill coming back."

He settled next to her. "Something to look forward to. Besides the overlook. It better be a spectacular view for all this work."

They sat for a few moments listening to the sounds of nature surrounding them. Without the rustling of their footsteps, they could hear insects chirping and creatures scurrying in the underbrush.

Cam replaced his water bottle in his backpack and stood to go. As he looked down at Olivia, he spied something move.

"Olivia," he said quietly. "Get up and move very slowly toward me."

Her eyes went wide and she turned her head to search around her. "What? What is it?"

He held out his hand, and she moved toward him, still looking behind her.

As he grasped her hand, he pulled her behind him and away from the rock. "A snake. I think it might have been a rattler."

Her shriek split the still air, reverberating through the forest, and she goose-stepped away from the rock, holding on to Cam like a human shield.

Cam's eyebrows drew together in a frown as he turned to face her. "He's probably more afraid of us than we are of him."

"No, nope, no way! I hate snakes!" She closed her eyes and shuddered.

"Well, I don't see him anymore. He probably crawled out to sun himself on the rock. But I think he's gone."

"He can have the rock. I'm out of here." She took off at a fast clip, leaving Cam behind.

As he caught up with her, he couldn't help laughing. "And here I thought you were a brave nature girl."

"Not when it comes to snakes."

He mused for a moment. "I think I have the perfect embarrassing thing to hold over your head."

"Don't you dare." She glared at him. "If you had any sense, you'd be scared to death of a rattlesnake, too. Have you seen the damage they can do?"

"Yes, but they generally don't bother people unless they are disturbed."

"Well, who knows how disturbed he was to see his rock occupied?" She continued briskly up the trail, talking over her shoulder.

"I . . . Oh wow! Olivia, turn around."

"What? Another snake?" Her eyes darted to the area around her feet.

"No. We're here. Look at that view."

The canopy of trees overhead gave way to a glorious valley below. It stretched out in front of them with distant hills and mountains rising toward the horizon. The plunging slopes leading down into the valley were covered with a hodgepodge of trees, some reaching straight to the sky, others bent and twisted in unusual shapes, the victims of cruel forces of nature. Blossoms covered some of the trees in a stunning display of pinks and whites, even those clinging desperately to the sides of the ridges. Dense vegetation sprinkled with wildflowers added layers of color to the rugged landscape. A small brook wound through the valley floor, its pristine waters sparkling in the sunlight. As if by design, a flat, rocky bluff, perfect for sitting and taking in the majestic scene, jutted out over the valley.

"Wow." Olivia swiveled her head to take in the panoramic view spread out before her.

"So, was the climb up here worth all the trouble?" Cam opened his backpack, pulled out a small blanket, and plopped down on the rocky bluff.

"I'll say," she breathed. "Well, except for the snake."

He chuckled. "Imagine this view in the fall with the leaves changing color."

She settled next to him. "It must be even more spectacular. Promise me we'll come back in the fall." She knew a commitment for a date several months from now presumed a lot about their relationship, but she didn't care. As things were going, the future appeared hopeful.

Cam nodded. "I promise."

Her heart fluttered, his promise igniting a spark within her of the deepening of their relationship. With his two words, he'd let her know he had no intentions of going anywhere.

"Hungry?" He began pulling out the makings of their picnic lunch.

She nodded, suddenly finding herself famished after the strenuous hike.

After lunch, Cam stretched out on his back, his arm over his eyes shading the sun.

"Don't fall asleep again," she teased.

"Not likely. This rock isn't the most comfortable place for a nap."

She sat with her knees drawn up to her chest, her arms wrapped around her legs. "Tell me your hopes and dreams."

He snorted. "Seriously? Do you want a book or the summarized version?"

"I'm serious, Cam. I want to know what stirs your heart. What you want out of life. Where you see yourself in ten years."

He sighed. "I think you know the answer to all those things. I want to be exactly what I am, doing exactly what I'm doing. Ranching is all I ever wanted to do from the time I was a kid on my uncle's ranch. I don't need anything more than that to be content."

She swallowed, noting he hadn't said anything about wanting a family to share his life with. "If you were so happy working with your uncle, why did you move here?"

It took a moment for him to respond. "It was time for a change. Now, how about you? What are your hopes and dreams?"

He had avoided answering the question by diverting the attention back to her. A little warning sounded in her brain, but she chose to ignore it. Maybe she could reroute the conversation later. "I see myself doing what I'm doing, too. Working with horses is all I've ever wanted."

"Did you ever think about going to veterinary school?"

She shook her head, but he probably couldn't see with his eyes covered. "I'm not smart enough."

At that, he removed his arm from his forehead, sat up, and looked at her. "Don't ever sell yourself short. You're plenty smart, among several other great qualities that make you so amazing."

"Is it wrong not to be more ambitious?"

His soft eyes locked onto hers. "You're plenty ambitious. Not everyone can do what you do."

She considered her next words carefully. "Am I ambitious enough for you?"

His forehead wrinkled in confusion, then his shoulders sagged. "Oh, my sweet, Olivia. You're perfect just the way you are." He gathered her into his arms. "You're everything a man could ever want."

She had to keep pushing. "A man like you?"

For his response, he pulled her into a long kiss. "Does that answer your question?" he asked, after breaking the kiss.

"Yes and no, Cam. I need to hear you say the words." She lowered her eyes, her heart hammering away against her ribcage. "You see, I'm falling for you and I don't want to get my hopes up and my heart broken again."

"I would never do that to you," he murmured against her hair. "You see, I'm falling in love with you, too."

Fireworks exploded in her chest. She threw her

arms around his neck and hugged him so tightly she couldn't breathe. She finally pulled back and looked into his eyes. "Now what?"

He laughed. "We take it one day at a time."

One day at a time. She could do that. Resting her head against his chest, she sat quietly mulling over his words. She could see a future with this man, one who seemed perfectly matched to her in every way. Still, she had to be careful not to rush ahead.

She didn't know how long they sat before she noticed the angle of the sun shifting. He kissed the top of her head and said, "We'd better head back."

Glancing at her watch, Olivia was surprised to see that several hours had passed since they'd started their hike. She began gathering up the remains of their picnic, stuffing everything into the two backpacks.

When they stood to go, he pulled her to him again. "One last look," he said, gazing out over the valley.

She wished she could freeze this moment in time. Everything was so perfect. He bent his head and sought her lips once more before starting down the path.

Going down seemed more treacherous than climbing up. The downward slope combined with a slippery forest floor made the journey difficult. Olivia let Cam lead the way, providing a steadying hand to her as they descended. But when they passed the rock where they'd encountered the snake, Olivia bypassed Cam and quickened her pace. As she did so, her heel caught on a root, and she went tumbling down the incline, landing hard at the bottom.

"Olivia!" he cried. Cam scurried down the trail as fast as he could safely manage.

She sat up, brushing dirt and mud from her arms and legs. "I'm fine. I didn't hurt anything but my pride."

He took her arms and pulled her to her feet. "Are you sure?"

Olivia tried to wipe the debris from her rear end, her hands coming away covered in mud and leaves. She rubbed them on the front of her jeans. "I must look a sight."

Only then did he laugh. "I can honestly say you've looked better." He reached up and wiped a smudge from her cheek.

"Great," she grumbled. "Now you've got *two* embarrassing things to hold over my head."

"Yeah." He grinned. "I sure do."

Chapter Nineteen

Although they'd tried to take things one day at a time, Cam wanted to be with Olivia every minute. He'd tried to rationally examine the pros and cons of a serious relationship with Olivia and couldn't see any reason not to tread into deeper waters. Each time they were together, his heart danced with a joy he had never experienced. His thoughts became consumed with her, often daydreaming about her when he needed to focus on his work. He lay awake at night musing about what it would be like to share his life with her and how nice it would be not to have to leave her at the door to her apartment and come home to an empty bed. Every detail about her seared itself into his memory—how her smile lit up her face, her softness contrasted with her strength, how appealing she looked whether in a dress or her jeans and boots. Thinking about his world without her in it made him feel adrift, as though she were his anchor. He finally understood how someone could be so intertwined with another person, as though they were somehow incomplete without the other.

They took long rides around the ranch, their laughter drowning out the hoofbeats of the horses, ignoring the knowing smiles of Ben, Darcy, and Ricky. Cam taught her more about his job in taking care of the cattle, and she enthusiastically worked alongside him in her free time. He didn't even mind the teasing from Ben and Ricky. In turn, he helped her saddle up horses for her trail rides and riding lessons and helped her stow everything away when her work ended. They walked through the town poking through shops and museums they'd never explored before. On several occasions, they drove to the Tetons, hiked new trails, and picnicked along the lakes. He visited her church and she visited his, with the unspoken understanding that eventually if things continued to move forward, they would have to choose where to worship together.

~

On her day off, Olivia called Cam at work. "Hey, cowboy, what're you doing tonight?"

His deep chuckle sounded in her ear. "Depends. What do you have in mind?"

"I'm cooking dinner."

"What?" The unmistakable tone of surprise in his voice made her smile.

"Don't sound so shocked. I've cooked for you before."

"Yeah, grilled cheese sandwiches and canned soup. I don't think tuna salad counts as cooking."

"Well, you knew what you were getting into. I told you from the beginning I couldn't cook."

"Yes, you did. And I fell for you anyway. So, to what do I owe this sudden impulse of domesticity?"

She hesitated. She didn't want to come right out and say that if they got even *more* serious—the implications of which she was not yet ready to name—

she would have to learn to cook. They couldn't continue eating out all the time or eating sandwiches at her place.

"Do I have to have a reason?" she asked.

"Yes. You've piqued my curiosity."

"Let's just say I want to do something nice for you."

He laughed. "From the way you've described your cooking skills in the past, I'm not sure whether to be flattered or worried."

"Fine. That's what I get for trying to do something special for you." Although she pretended to be hurt, the smile in her voice gave her away.

"Okay. I'm flattered. What time?"

"Six?"

"See you then. I'll pick up some Peptol-bismol on the way." He disconnected before she could reply.

The smile disappeared from her face and her heart began to stutter. What had she just done? She punched in another number and held her breath until the familiar voice answered.

"Mom? I'm in big trouble! I need help!"

"Why? What's wrong?" Her mother's voice raised an octave.

"I just told Cam I'd cook dinner for him tonight. I don't know what to make."

Her mother's relieved sigh hissed in her ear. "Olivia. For heaven's sake, you scared me to death. I thought something terrible had happened."

"If I end up giving him food poisoning, something terrible *will* happen."

"All right. Calm down. It's not like I didn't try to teach you how to cook, but you were always too preoccupied with your horses to bother learning."

"I know, Mom, just tell me what to do *now*."

"Okay. I'll email you my lasagna recipe. It's easy to make and should impress your young man. You can pick up some French bread and a premixed salad."

~

Olivia sat across from Cam at her small kitchen table and watched him lift a forkful of lasagna to his mouth. Too nervous to taste the dinner she'd labored over, she waited, her heart in her throat, for him to render a verdict. He chewed for what seemed like a long time before swallowing, following up with a large gulp of water.

"Well?"

He cleared his throat. "It's, um . . . different."

"Different? What does that mean?"

He wiped his mouth with his napkin, then buttered a slice of bread. "See what *you* think."

She dropped her eyes to her plate and cut off a corner of her lasagna with the side of her fork. It seemed like she was having to saw through the noodles, but she finally managed to get the bite free. She tasted it, feeling the texture of the noodles against her tongue before biting into them.

"Oh! It's terrible. The noodles are chewy." She forced the bite down her throat and looked at the congealed glob of cheese on the top of the casserole. "And the cheese didn't melt like it was supposed to."

"What kind of noodles did you use?" he asked, bravely attacking another bite.

"The 'ready-to-bake.' I thought it sounded easier than boiling noodles."

"Are you sure?" he asked around a mouthful of

food.

"I think so." She hopped up and went to the kitchen trash, pulling out the box. "Oh. I guess not. I must have picked up the wrong box."

He swallowed again and chased the bolus down with water. "That would explain it. And the cheese?"

"No fat mozzarella. I thought it sounded healthier than regular."

He shook his head. "No fat cheese won't melt."

She covered her face with her hands. "The dinner's a disaster."

"Not entirely. We still have bread and salad."

She moaned. "I wanted so badly to impress you with my cooking."

He laughed. "You did. I'm impressed."

Removing her hands from her face, she glared at him. "That's not funny. I tried really hard."

Cam rose from his seat and knelt in front of her. Taking her hands in both of his, he brought them to his lips. "I know, sweetheart. And you don't know how much it means to me."

"What are we going to do if I can't cook? We can't go on eating sandwiches forever."

He pulled her to her feet. "That's simple. Marry a man who can cook."

Her breath caught, and he quickly released her hands, turning back to the table.

Without meeting her eyes, he said, "So, do you want to keep the rest of this?"

Too stunned to reply, she shook her head.

He carried the lasagna pan to the counter, where he scraped the remainder into the trash. "Do you want to go out and get something to eat?"

"Uh, sure, if you do."

Cam wrapped up the rest of the bread and put the salad in the refrigerator. "Okay, grab your purse."

Olivia waited in suspense the rest of the evening for Cam to work the conversation back to the "M" word, but he never did. Slightly disappointed, she realized it must have been a slip of the tongue. He'd behaved quite awkwardly around her the rest of the night—not looking directly at her, talking about inconsequential matters, laughing too loudly at things that weren't funny. When they returned to her apartment, he'd given her a quick peck on the lips and said he had to get up early, leaving her sad and a little frustrated. Perhaps it was premature to be talking about marriage, but she had hopes they were headed in that direction. Even if he hadn't meant to bring up marriage, did he have to act so strange about his slip-up? What now? Were they back to awkwardness and tiptoeing around their feelings?

Chapter Twenty

Cam mentally kicked himself for blurting out the words, "Marry a man who can cook." If that wasn't a lead-in to a proposal, what was? It wasn't as though he hadn't been thinking along those lines in an abstract sort of way. But thinking about marriage and acting on it were two different things. He wasn't sure he was quite ready to take things to that level. Now he had hurt Olivia's feelings over the dinner, as well as get her hopes up and dash them to pieces. If they could only find their way back to where they were before he stuck his big foot in his mouth.

He tossed and turned all night berating himself and wondering how to fix things. He didn't want to lose Olivia, but he also didn't want to string her along with false promises for something he wasn't ready to deliver. But the more he thought about it, would an engagement be out of the question? A long engagement, obviously. Rushing headlong into marriage at this stage of their relationship would be foolish. Regardless of his feelings for her, he had to lead with his head, not his emotions. Marriage involved a lifelong commitment and, despite the fact he couldn't imagine a more perfect soul mate, he knew there were bits and pieces of their individual lives that they still didn't know about each other, one in particular that he still couldn't bear to share with her yet. He tried to pray about the confusion in his mind but sensed no peace.

Despite his reluctance to discuss his personal life with others, he needed wisdom from godly men—men who had been where he was not so long ago. He waited until they'd completed the morning rounds before they split up to tend to their individual chores. The fence in the upper pasture could wait a little longer.

Swallowing his pride, he said, "Guys, could I talk with you for a minute?"

Ben and Ricky stopped their horses and turned to him, all teasing erased from their faces.

"What's up, buddy?" asked Ben.

Cam took in a deep breath and related what he'd said to Olivia the night before. "I'm wrestling with the uncertainty of wanting to take that next step and, at the same time, being afraid. How can I be sure?"

The other two men exchanged glances. Then Ben spoke. "It's understandable. I had similar doubts about Darcy, especially after my broken engagement to Jolene. I didn't want to make another mistake. But the more I was with Darcy, the more I couldn't picture my life without her." He looked at Ricky to continue.

"Well, you know my story," said Ricky. "I could never see myself with another woman after my first wife, Lily, died. And I was pretty angry at God for taking her. Then He put Kendra in my path." He stopped and chuckled. "Literally. I kept stumbling over the woman. Then one night, God spoke to me loud and clear." Ricky's gaze settled off in the distance.

"You never told us about that," said Cam.

Ricky shook his head. "I guess not. It was such a powerful, overwhelming experience. It still gives me chills when I think about it."

"I didn't know anything about that, either," said Ben. "Can you share it with us?"

Ricky blew out a breath. "He didn't speak audibly, of course, but I heard His voice in my soul as plainly as if He had spoken aloud. He said, *'Lily's happy. She's with Me. She would want you to be happy, too.'* I guess if that's not confirmation, nothing is."

Cam mulled over Ricky's revelation. Although startling in its clarity, God had given Cam no such revelation. "That's an incredible experience. I wish God would speak to me that clearly."

"He speaks to each of us in His own way," said Ben. "If you continue to pray about His will, He will eventually reveal it to you."

Cam nodded. He respected his two friends and appreciated how they'd dealt with similar doubts, but Cam wasn't trying to protect himself from a broken heart like Ben or Ricky. He hadn't suffered the death of a spouse or the messiness of a failed engagement to the wrong woman. He had no issue with God, but God hadn't given him the peace and the assurance to move forward.

"Let me give you another piece of unsolicited advice, bro," said Ricky. "If there's anything you're holding back, you need to get it out in the open. I almost lost Kendra because I wasn't completely honest with her about my past."

Cam's head snapped up. Bingo. Subconsciously, he'd known the answer all along. At some point, he had to tell Olivia about what had happened with Finn.

"Thanks, guys," he said. "You've given me plenty to think about."

"Anytime, buddy," said Ben. "We're always here for you."

"I'm going to get to work on that fence. See you later." Cam gently pulled the reins to the left and nudged his horse in that direction, his thoughts swirling through his head in a kaleidoscope of changing pictures.

Much as he didn't want to, he relived that fateful day in his head like a bad movie.

~

"Are you sure you don't mind watching Finn?" Annette asked for the third time.

Cam took in the anxious expression on his younger sister's face. She'd been through so much in the past year, and he just wanted to wave a magic wand and make all the pain go away.

"Sis, you know I don't mind. I love the little Finnster. He's my best bud."

The worry lines creasing her too-young face tugged at his heart.

He closed the small gap between them and hugged her tightly. "It'll be all right. We'll get through this."

A sniffle sounded against his shoulder. "I should have listened to everybody. I never should have married Joel."

He felt hot tears against his neck. "Sis, you were eighteen and in love. You were hardly old enough to know better."

She clung to him for a minute before stepping

back and brushing her hand under her reddened eyes. "But look at the mess I've made of everything."

He tucked a strand of dark hair behind her ear. "Shh. You didn't make the mess. Joel did."

She shook her head, her eyes full of pain and bewilderment. "But he was never like this in high school. It wasn't until Finn was born that he . . ."

Cam had listened to his sister's reiteration of Joel's betrayal and her inability to explain the change in his behavior many times over the past several months. She still couldn't seem to grasp that marriage and fatherhood at such a young age had weighed him down with a responsibility too big for him to carry on his shoulders. While Annette had basked in the joy of being a young wife and mother, Joel had become more like a caged animal. Selfishly happy in her own life, she'd failed to see, or perhaps overlooked, his growing discontent until he'd begun lashing out with verbal and physical abuse. Then came the drinking and the other women.

Ironically, although Joel didn't want to be tied down, his male ego wouldn't tolerate the idea of Annette leaving him. She ignored the pleas of her family and friends to escape her dangerous situation until the night he broke Finn's arm. That's when she finally took out the restraining order against her husband, moved back to her parents' house with Finn, and filed for divorce.

Annette reached for a tissue on the coffee table and loudly blew her nose. "The daycare will have an opening for Finn next week, even if Mom and Dad aren't back from Grandma's." Their grandfather had died a month before, and their parents were helping their grandmother move to an assisted living facility. Cleaning out a lifetime in the house they'd lived in for fifty years was no small task.

"I know, I know. You've told me." He smiled at her, hoping to ease her burden.

"I just wish I didn't have to work—"

"But you do. I'm off today and tomorrow before the weekend. I've got this."

She took a faltering breath. "Okay. He's still asleep, but when he wakes up—"

"I know. Feed him. Brush his teeth. Get him dressed. Don't let him watch too much TV." He handed her her purse and her jacket. "It looks like it's going to be a nice day. Maybe we'll go to the park."

Her shoulders relaxed. "He'd like that. I can't thank you enough—"

Cam put an arm around her and ushered her to the door. "That's what big brothers are for. Now get to work. You don't want to be fired for being late."

She gave him a half-hearted smile and a kiss on the cheek. "What would I do without you?"

"Maybe this will make up for the time I blew up your Barbie doll with firecrackers."

She laughed and smacked his arm. "I still haven't forgiven you for that, you know."

His eyebrows shot up in mock surprise. "Even though Mom and Dad made me buy you *two* replacement Barbies to atone for my sin?"

She raised her chin. "That one was my favorite." She disappeared out the door, stepping lighter than he'd seen in a long time.

~

The day had turned out to be perfect, in the upper

sixties with soft sunlight filtering through cottony clouds in the pale blue sky. The coolness of the early morning gave way to soothing warmth as the sun rose higher. Finn had slept in late, thrilled when he awoke to find his uncle waiting for him. Cam had made pancakes, Finn's favorite, then suggested they walk to the park down the street. Cam chuckled at Finn's whoop of delight. It took so little to make the child happy. Cam wondered, fleetingly, if he'd ever experience the joy of being a father. So far, there had been no woman he'd been attracted to enough to consider marrying and starting a family with. And he never wanted to go down the disastrous road Annette had walked by marrying the wrong person. But he sure loved his little nephew. Maybe he'd have to settle for being cool Uncle Cam. Finn needed a strong, loving male role model in his life.

The almost-three-year-old skipped to the park beside Cam, chattering away in his cheerful childish voice. Cam couldn't remember ever being so content. They came to the gate surrounding the park, and Finn bounced up and down until Cam managed to flip up the latch. Then he took off like a racehorse out of the starting gate toward the slides. Cam settled on a bench and watched the boy play in utter innocent abandon. Like a little monkey, he climbed easily up the ladder leading to the slide, going down, then running back to do it all over again. Cam grew tired just watching the expenditure of toddler energy.

He tipped his head back to the sun, letting its comforting rays spill over him in welcome respite. It had been a busy week at his uncle's ranch, what with several calvings and the inevitable complications that followed some of them. Before his eyes drifted closed, he forced them open, following Finn's movements as he went down the slide, again and again. Cam's phone pinged in his pocket. Frowning, he pulled it out and opened his text messages. Drat. Another problem at the ranch. The new ranch hand was by himself this morning, something Cam had been a little concerned about, but Uncle John had assured him the kid could handle things while he had to go into town on business.

Cam read through the text, debating on whether he needed to load up Finn and head out there or if he could simply advise the kid. It sounded like one of the cows might have milk fever, a condition in which the calcium level in the blood dropped, causing the cow to go down. He quickly tapped a reply with his two thumbs. The ranch hand had assisted him a couple of times in treating milk fever. He told him where to find the bottles of calcium, needles, and tubing to administer the intravenous solution. After a few seconds, the kid sent another text with more questions. A sigh escaped Cam's lips, as he replied. Again, within a few seconds, another text appeared. Cam groaned. If it was a milk fever, it shouldn't wait until his uncle returned. He typed, "I'm on my way," then tucked the phone back in his pocket.

Getting to his feet, he scanned the area where Finn had been playing. "Finn? Hey, bud, we've got to go out to the ranch." His nephew was no longer by the slides. "Finn?" He raised his voice and took several steps toward the slides, shading his eyes with the edge of his hand against the glaring sunlight. He looked around toward the monkey bars and the swings, not seeing the dark-haired little boy in the red-striped shirt.

Picking up his pace, he began walking the perimeter of the park calling for his nephew. The boy had to be here somewhere. He couldn't open the gate and get out by himself. As his brisk strides turned into jogging, panic began to seize his gut. His pulse ratcheted as fear wrapped strangling tendrils around his heart. He asked every adult he passed, "Have you seen a little boy wearing a red-striped shirt?" They all replied in the negative, although a couple of people joined him in the search.

Could Finn be hiding? Playing a game? "Finn! If you're hiding, please come out. I mean it." Cam scoured behind every bush and obstacle where a small child could crouch. "This isn't funny, Finn, come out now!"

"Should we call the police?" asked one of the mothers, grasping her small daughter's hand firmly in her own.

Cam's throat closed with fear and his brain froze. "Finn!" he bellowed.

"I'm calling the police," the woman said, reaching for her cellphone.

Another woman approached him. "Are you looking for a kid about three years old? Dark hair?"

Relief flooded through Cam's veins. "Yes! Have you seen him?"

The woman's brows furrowed. "I saw him leaving the park about ten minutes ago with a man."

Full-blown terror replaced the brief sensation of relief. "What did he look like?"

The woman bit her lip, obviously trying to recall. "Um, tall, maybe six feet, close-cropped sandy hair."

Joel.

"I'm sorry. I didn't think anything about it. The boy didn't appear upset—"

"Did you see which way they went?"

She shook her head. "I'm sorry, I didn't."

The first woman said, "The police are on their way."

Cam didn't reply as he raced to the gate, hoping to catch a glimpse of Joel and Finn walking down the street, but he knew it was probably pointless. If Joel had been planning to kidnap his son, he would have parked close by for a quick getaway. He must have been watching them, stalking them, just waiting for the right moment. Sure enough, the street was deserted. *Think, Cam, think. What kind of vehicle did Joel drive?* He knew that was a long shot as well, as he hadn't seen Joel in over a year, and Joel could have acquired a new vehicle. Annette. He had to call Annette. But how was he going to tell her he had lost her son?

Chapter Twenty-One

Olivia missed Brian. It had been several weeks since she'd seen her nephew, and she wondered how he was getting along with his new family. She'd never figured on not being a part of his life after Martha died. But there was really nobody she could call to check on his welfare. It seemed as quickly as he had come into her life, he had been taken away. She'd never expected to fall so in love with the little boy in such a short time. Every time she saw a small child, her heart tore a little. Perhaps she should have tried harder to figure out a way to raise him. Other people managed as single parents. But even her mother, having raised Olivia as a single mother, agreed with her decision. It was better for Brian to have a stable home with two loving parents, even if they weren't blood kin. Fortunately, she had her work and Cam to take her mind off her loss.

But she hadn't seen Cam at work the next day after the disastrous evening before. He hadn't been hanging around the barn waiting for her like he usually did. A pang of sadness pierced her heart at the thought that perhaps Cam was pulling away from her. She was tempted to call or text him, but something stopped her. Cam might need time to process what he'd inadvertently said, and she didn't want to appear pushy. Yet, he'd admitted his feelings for her, so part of her didn't understand his distancing himself. Maybe she was overreacting. Maybe he just worked late. But she noticed Ben and Ricky putting their horses away at the usual time.

When she didn't see him the following day, she cornered Ben before he started his morning rounds.

"Cam just took a few days off," Ben told her. "He said he needed to clear his head."

Worry clutched at her insides, sending doubt racing through her blood.

Ben removed his hat and gave her a warm, reassuring smile. "Don't look so upset. Give him some time. Everything will be okay."

Heat rose in her cheeks. How much did Ben know? What had Cam told him? She swallowed around the lump in her throat and nodded.

Ben replaced his hat and gave her a wave as he nudged Kimber into a trot. Olivia took a long, slow breath and tried to quiet the tangled thoughts echoing in her brain. As she turned to go into the barn, her phone rang. She dug the phone from her jeans pocket and glanced at a number she didn't recognize. Probably a telemarketer. She wavered between answering it and letting it go to voicemail, then swiped the answer button.

"Hello?" She knew her voice didn't sound very welcoming, but as downcast as she felt, she didn't care. Especially if it was a telemarketer.

"Miss Anderson?" came a woman's deep voice.

"Yes?"

"This is Mrs. Chadwick with the Department of Children and Families in Salt Lake City."

Olivia's pulse quickened. What would the DCF be calling her about? Was something wrong with Brian?

"Yes?" Fear gripped her with icy fingers.

"We have your nephew, Brian, in foster care. He—"

"What? Why is Brian in foster care? What happened to the family who was supposed to adopt him?" Olivia fired off the questions in rapid succession.

A long pause ensued. "I'm afraid that's why I'm calling, Miss Anderson. The situation with the adoptive family didn't work out and—"

"What? Why? What happened?" How could anyone not love Brian? Olivia ran a hand over her forehead where a headache had started to throb.

The woman sighed. "The parents' biological child couldn't adapt to having another child in the home. It became too difficult for them to manage."

Olivia's heart hammered, sending blood thrumming through her ears. "So, what does this mean?"

"Unfortunately, you are Brian's only relative. If you are unable or unwilling to take him, he will remain in foster care until he can hopefully be adopted."

"I'll be there to get him tomorrow." She didn't hear any of what Mrs. Chadwick said after that. God had given her another chance. He meant for her to have Brian. They would make it work.

~

Olivia rose before dawn to make the five-hour drive to Salt Lake City. Her emotions waffled between elated and scared to death. She would have to get a bigger apartment. Brian couldn't sleep on the couch forever. She would have to arrange for daycare or preschool. Was he old enough for preschool? What about in the afternoons when she worked? How was she going to pay for all this? How was Brian coping with the loss of his mother? How would she help him through his grieving process? Would he need counseling? Did counselors even work with kids that young?

She spent an hour of the drive praying for wisdom and patience. Being an aunt for a few hours was one thing. Being a full-time guardian of a small child was another. She prayed for God to work out the details. Surely His hand was in this change of events. But He was handing her the challenge of her life.

She arrived before lunch, her stomach in knots. As she got out of her car and stretched her legs, she looked up at the foreboding, industrial-looking brick building in front of her that featured little aesthetic appeal. No grass provided a contrast between the hot asphalt parking lot and the concrete walkway. No potted plants graced the entry. The small windows appeared like tiny slits in the vast expanse of brick, offering only a narrow view of the outside. Of course, there was nothing much to see outside, besides the ugly parking lot. Olivia wondered how much heartache these walls had seen, from the frightened children removed from parents unable to care for them, to parents sobbing to be reunited with their children, promising the world. Some would do anything to clean up their act. Others wouldn't or couldn't. Then there were the foster parents fighting to protect the children in their care and prospective adoptive parents, some of whom would have their dreams shattered when adoptions fell through.

Olivia squared her shoulders and pulled the heavy glass door open. The oppressive atmosphere surrounded her the minute she stepped into the recirculated stale air of the over-chilled lobby. She looked around at people waiting in hard, plastic chairs, their expressions blank. A lone woman sat at a reception desk to the right, a telephone tucked against her shoulder held to her left ear. Olivia rubbed the goosebumps from her arms and approached the desk. The woman scowled at her as though she were intruding. Olivia waited patiently while the woman wrapped up a long-winded conversation.

"Yes?" she snapped.

"I'm Olivia Anderson. I'm here to see Mrs. Chadwick."

Without replying, the woman picked up the phone again, punched a button, and announced Olivia's arrival.

"Have a seat." The woman jerked her head toward the myriad of other people in the lobby.

"Thank you."

Without replying, the woman returned her attention to her computer monitor.

Olivia settled onto a chair beside a woman who fiddled with her phone, ignoring everything around her. Olivia was just as grateful the woman didn't try to engage her in conversation. Periodically, the locked door to the inner sanctum opened and someone from the lobby was called back. Olivia glanced at her watch, wondering what was taking so long. She thought about asking the surly receptionist but decided against it. Although her stomach churned like an angry sea, it also rumbled with hunger. She'd been too nervous to eat breakfast, and she realized the coffee she'd swigged on the long drive had long since worn off.

Finally, the door opened and a tall, pleasant-looking middle-aged woman wearing horn-rimmed glasses and holding several files of paperwork called her name.

She extended her hand and said, "I apologize for the wait. I'm Mrs. Chadwick."

Some of the butterflies in Olivia's stomach disappeared as the warm, capable-appearing woman turned and ushered her deeper into the cavernous hallway. Their footsteps echoed on the cheap tile flooring, bouncing off the drab, gray-painted walls on either side. Overhead fluorescent lights gave an unnatural brightness to the overall dismal interior. Mrs. Chadwick stopped about halfway down the hall and motioned for Olivia to precede her into a small, cluttered office.

"Before Brian gets here, we need to go over several forms." The older woman sank into a squeaky swivel chair next to her desk and invited Olivia to sit in the only other chair facing her.

At the mention of Brian's name, Olivia's heart fluttered with joyful anticipation, and she wanted to dispense with the paperwork as quickly as possible. She listened as Mrs. Chadwick went over all the documents, but she had to focus hard to keep her attention from drifting to the moment she would finally see Brian.

"His mother's trust left more than enough money to adequately care for Brian," said Mrs. Chadwick, as she passed over a ream of papers.

Money? The realization that she wouldn't have to scrape together every spare nickel and dime to provide for the child allayed one of her many concerns. Of course, Martha had provided for Brian. Why hadn't Olivia thought of that? One less thing to worry about. Mrs. Chadwick gave her the paperwork to take to her lawyer—okay, now she had to find a lawyer—in Wyoming. She also gave her paperwork to file in Wyoming for legal custody of Brian and information about moving toward adoption.

Olivia signed form after form, some of which she scanned, others for which she relied on Mrs. Chadwick's word. At one point, another young woman came into the office and notarized several documents. Just as they finished up, the telephone on the desk buzzed, and Mrs. Chadwick reported that Brian was waiting for them in the lobby.

Olivia had to restrain herself from running out of the office. Her world was about to change in a huge way, but she couldn't wait. As Mrs. Chadwick pushed open the door to the lobby, Olivia spied her nephew sitting in a plastic chair, his short legs swinging back and forth.

"Brian!" she cried, squatting in front of him.

"Aunt O!" The boy jumped from his seat and flew into her arms. She held him tightly against her, overcome with the pure joy of touching him again. "I knew you'd come back. I told them you'd come back."

She released him and peered intently into his shining, dark eyes. "I'm here, Brian. I'll never leave you again." Brushing his dark hair from his eyes, she stood, clasping his small hand.

Another woman stepped forward. "I'm Norma Wiggins, Brian's social worker. I've got all his things in my van if you'd like to follow me."

Thankfully, Norma had Brian's car seat because Olivia hadn't thought of that. A shadow of doubt crossed her mind, yet again, wondering what else she'd failed to think of. No matter. She would figure it out. They loaded up every square inch of her trunk and the inside of her car, and she deliberated where she was going to put all of Brian's stuff. Looking for a bigger apartment moved to the top of her priority list. At last, they were on their way, Brian chattering nonstop.

Olivia swung into a drive-through fast food restaurant where she ordered chicken nuggets and fries for Brian and a double cheeseburger for herself. Her hunger pangs had complained with a vengeance during her couple of hours at the DCF, and she gobbled her burger without thinking of the stomach ache she would incur later.

"I'm glad I'm going to live with you, Aunt O," said Brian around a mouthful of fries. "Wesley was mean to me."

She glanced into the rearview mirror. "Who's Wesley?"

"He's the Smith's little boy. He's six. He hit me and pushed me and took my toys."

Her heart sunk for the pain Brian had endured over the past few weeks, first with losing his mother, then being in a home with another child who bullied him. "I'm sorry, Brian, that wasn't very nice of him. But it's just you and me now. No Wesley."

"Good. Do you have a dog?"

She laughed at the way his mind switched gears

so suddenly. "No, but I work on a ranch with lots of horses. And there's a dog on the ranch named Mac."

"Horses?" His childish voice rose in excitement. "Can I see them?

"Yes, Brian, I'll take you to the ranch to see the horses. I'll even teach you to ride a horse. Would you like that?"

"I never rode a horse before."

"Well, you'll be a cowboy in no time."

"I love you, Aunt O."

Warmth surged through her veins. "I love you, too."

Before they reached the interstate, Brian fell fast asleep.

Chapter Twenty-Two

It took a while to get Brian settled down once they reached Olivia's apartment, but after dinner and a bath, he finally climbed under the covers on the sofa, surrounded by a troop of stuffed animals. Olivia sat in the dim glow of the nightlight watching him sleep, her heart full to overflowing. With her mind skittering in all directions with everything she had to do, she finally crawled into bed but lay tossing and turning. The chime of her phone startled her.

A text. From Cam! "Are you awake?"

She sat up and flipped on the lamp on her nightstand. "Yes," she typed back.

A moment later, his ringtone sounded. She pressed the answer call button. "Cam? I'm so glad to hear from you. I was worried."

A soft chuckle sounded in her ear. "I'm sorry, I didn't mean to worry you. I was hoping you'd still be up because I have some things I wanted to talk with you about."

Her pulse began to race. This was what Kyle had said before he broke up with her. She held her breath, unable to respond.

At her silence, he continued. "I've been doing a lot of thinking over the past few days. First of all, I want to apologize for my behavior the other night. I was . . . well, conflicted about some things, and I know my mind was elsewhere. But I want you to know I love you."

She let out her breath. Okay, this didn't sound like breaking up. "I love you, too," she whispered. "I've missed you."

"I've missed you, too. I've come to realize just how much I enjoy being with you and how well we fit together."

"I can't wait to see you, Cam. I've got a surprise for you." She didn't want to tell him about Brian on the phone. She wanted to see his eyes light up when he saw Brian.

"A surprise, huh? Now you've got me curious. What is it?"

She laughed. "If I tell you, it won't be a surprise. You'll just have to wait and see."

"That's hardly fair to spring something like that on me and leave me dangling." He paused. "But I have a surprise for you, too."

"You do? What?"

She heard him draw a long breath. "Actually, it's something I want to tell you."

"What?"

After another long pause, he said, "I want to tell you that I can cook."

For a moment, confusion clouded the meaning behind his words. "What did you say?"

"I said I can cook, Olivia."

Her heart skipped a beat, then began an erratic

cadence. "Are you saying what I think you're saying?"

His response was a soft chuckle. "It's probably better to talk about this in person. Over the phone is too impersonal. Besides, I have something else I need to tell you first."

"Cam, you can't—"

"How about I come by in the morning? Can you take off tomorrow?"

She had already arranged to take a few days off to get Brian settled. "Yes."

"Good. I'll see you around nine."

"Whatever you say."

"Goodnight." He disconnected.

Olivia sat holding the phone, her heart pounding like a jackhammer in her chest. If Cam had just proposed to her, it was the strangest marriage proposal she had ever heard of. But she'd take it.

Chapter Twenty-Three

Cam disconnected the call and reached over to his night table, retrieving a small velvet box. He flipped the lid and gazed intently at the small diamond solitaire nestled inside. Would Olivia like it? Would she rather pick out her own ring? Was it too small? A bigger ring would look out of place on Olivia's delicate finger. But a prickle of anxiety traveled up his spine. The small diamond was all he could afford, but didn't women prefer big diamonds? What if she didn't like it? Worse yet, what if she said no? She wouldn't say no, would she? They loved each other. They were right for each other. Of course, she wouldn't say no.

Was he rushing things? The engagement could be as long as she wanted. Women needed time to prepare for a wedding. *A wedding.* Visions of Bill and Audrey's wedding ran through his mind's eye, and he remembered how uncomfortable he had been. How uncomfortable Olivia had been. He didn't want people to be uncomfortable at his wedding. Panic threatened to derail his plan. Maybe they could secretly elope to the courthouse. But, no, Olivia would want a large wedding. Didn't every woman? Sweat beaded on his forehead. He hadn't thought beyond proposing to what the next few months would entail. Would Olivia turn into a Bridezilla? He willed his shallow breathing to steady. Men went through periods of engagement all the time. Ben and Ricky had survived. So would he. But how he wished they could skip over all the hoopla and already be married and live the rest of their lives together.

But before he did anything else, he needed to tell her about Finn.

~

After a largely sleepless night, Cam stood at Olivia's door, his hands shaking. He had never done anything like this before. His confidence from the previous night ebbed in the harsh reality of the morning's light. He took a deep breath through his nose, plastered a smile on his face, and knocked on her door. He fingered the ring box in his pocket while he waited.

She flung open the door, a big smile lightening up her face, and moved into his arms. Suddenly all his fears vanished. Or, most of them, anyway. His courage returned when he bent to kiss her, after being apart for several days. She pulled him into her living room and shut the door.

He sank onto the couch, momentarily perplexed by the wad of blankets, pillows, and stuffed animals. Olivia plopped down next to him, her face expectant and excited. He fiddled with the ring box again and turned to her.

"Olivia, I—"

Just as the words formed on his tongue, the bathroom door opened with a bang, and a young boy came running across the room. "Mr. Cam!"

Cam froze. Olivia gathered Brian into her lap, grinning. "I told you I had a surprise."

Suddenly speechless, Cam's eyes darted between the two. Then he cleared his throat. "I see Brian's visiting. That's nice."

"Not visiting, Mr. Cam. I live here now!" exclaimed the excited little boy.

Cam felt the blood drain from his face. He looked to Olivia for confirmation.

"That's my surprise." Merriment danced in her eyes. "I'm adopting Brian."

Cam's vision blurred, and the blood roaring through his ears muffled the sounds in the room. His pulse spiked, his heartbeat erratic and thready, and his throat constricted. He recognized all too well the panic attack taking over his body and fought to catch his breath.

"Isn't that great?"

He could feel her eyes on him, but her face had become indistinct and out of focus.

"Cam, are you okay? What's wrong?"

The room seemed to spin. He rested his elbows on his knees and put his head in his hands. This couldn't be happening. He couldn't take on the responsibility for someone else's child again. He would never survive if something happened to another child. Finn's kidnapping still haunted him and plagued him with nightmares.

He slowly got to his feet, his vision clearing. Shaking his head, he said, "I can't do this, Olivia."

She moved Brian off her lap and stood with him. "Can't do what?"

"I can't have children," he said, his voice soft and raspy.

Her eyes searched his. "I don't understand."

"I can't have children," he repeated louder.

She swallowed and said, "That's okay, we—"

"No!" His tone was sharper than he'd intended, and he saw her flinch. "You *don't* understand! I don't mean I can't *physically* have children. I mean I can't *emotionally* have children."

He saw her forehead wrinkle in confusion, and as much as he wanted to take her into his arms and kiss away the fear he saw creeping into her eyes, he couldn't. He could not be with her if she had a child.

"I'm sorry, Olivia," he said, leaving her standing in the middle of the room, tears pooling in her eyes, as he hurried out the door.

Although his legs felt like heavy chains bound them, he took the stairs two at a time as he made his escape. Once in his truck, he paused to let his pulse slow down. *Stupid! Stupid! Of course Olivia would want children. What made you think she wouldn't? You never discussed this. You just assumed marriage to you would be enough for her. But how could she know? You never told her about Finn.*

He had been deluding himself this whole time. Somewhere, in the back of his mind, he had always known the truth, which was probably why he'd never gotten close to a woman before Olivia. No woman would want to marry him under the condition they wouldn't have children. It didn't matter how suited he and Olivia were for each other. Women wanted families. At least most women did. Overwhelming fatigue permeated his bones. He'd come so close, but he hadn't thought things all the way through. He thought he'd worked out all his doubts, and he had— about Olivia, anyway. But he'd never given her the chance to work out her doubts about him.

~

Stunned, Olivia remained rooted to the spot where she'd stood with Cam just a minute ago. What had just happened? Last night, she had been so sure that Cam had been proposing, in a roundabout way. And everything was fine until Brian came into the room. What was it about Brian that had suddenly freaked Cam out? Did he dislike children *that* much? She had seen him interact with some of the kids she taught, and he was always friendly, even teasing. Was it Brian he didn't like? How could anybody not like the adorable little boy sitting on her sofa, his little face contorted with confusion?

"Aunt O?"

Olivia swallowed her tears, not wanting to upset the child even more. Her heart had plummeted to her stomach, so it took a moment for her to compose herself. She forced a shaky smile and turned to him.

"Is Mr. Cam mad at me?"

Her shattered heart suddenly rose again to her chest, filled with a fierce, protective love toward the innocent little boy who had done nothing wrong. "Oh, no, sweetheart, no." She sat next to him and drew him close. Trying to steady her voice, she said, "I'm not sure what's wrong with Mr. Cam, but it has nothing to do with you."

Skepticism shone on his face. *Now is the time to be the adult in his life, Olivia.* "But you know what?" She forced gaiety into her tone. "You and I have a lot to do today, starting with breakfast. How about we go get a sausage biscuit, then we need to look for a bigger apartment. One where you can have your own room."

"Okay."

He still didn't look convinced that nothing amiss had happened, and Olivia delved back into her memory of when she was his age. She remembered when her father died and people kept telling her everything was okay when she knew it wasn't. But as badly as her heart hurt right now, her first priority had to be Brian. She could not afford to fall apart over Cam.

Chapter Twenty-Four

Cam's chaotic emotions made it difficult for him to concentrate the next day at the ranch. His few days off had carried him to the top of the rollercoaster—with a bright, happy future with the woman he loved—only to plunge him to the depths of hopelessness. He shouldn't have tried to change his course in life. Since his failure to keep Finn safe, he'd always known he was destined to be alone, with only himself to worry about. Taking on the responsibility for someone else, even Olivia, was just too scary.

"Hey, man, what's up with you today?" asked Ben, when Cam's mind had wandered off again. "I thought with all those days off, you got your head clear." Ben sat atop Malachi waiting to ride to the northern pasture. Cam stood beside Kimber, not yet in the saddle.

Cam squeezed his eyes shut and drew in a deep breath. "I did, but now I don't."

Ben squinted at him. "Okay, man, now you've lost me. Is it Olivia?"

Of course it was Olivia. Didn't every drama in a man's life begin with a woman? "Ben, she's adopting her nephew."

"Yeah, I know. So, what's the problem? Don't you like the kid?"

Cam hesitated. "Can we walk for a few minutes? I need to get something off my chest."

Ben eyed him strangely, but climbed down from his horse, holding the reins loosely in his hand.

They walked the horses several hundred feet before Cam spoke again. "It's something that happened a few years ago when I was babysitting for my nephew." He poured out the whole story, about how he had been responsible for taking care of Finn and how he'd been distracted by a text message, allowing Finn's father to abduct him from the park.

Ben took off his hat and wiped his hand across his sweaty brow. "Man, that had to be terrible."

Cam nodded. "You have no idea."

"But you got Finn back, right?"

"Yeah. Five days later." The fear that always arose every time Cam thought of those agonizing five days assaulted him as though the incident were fresh.

Ben loosened the grip on Malachi's reins so he could nibble on the lush grass, and Cam followed suit with Kimber. "Was he harmed?"

Cam shook his head. "No, thank God. But those five days were the worst in my life. Not only did I blame myself for what happened, but I worried constantly that Finn was hurt or worse. Joel didn't kidnap Finn because he wanted him. Joel was a vengeful man, and I wouldn't have put it past him to hurt Finn to get back at Annette."

"But you did get him back." Ben placed a hand on Cam's arm. "That's the important thing."

"No thanks to me. Annette still blames me. Our relationship hasn't been the same since." Cam looked off into the distance at a scene only he could see.

Ben made murmurs of understanding. "Where is Joel now?"

Cam stared at the mountains standing against the backdrop of the horizon, their peaks reaching toward the cloudless sky, but the beauty of the scene failed to register. "He was in prison. Last we heard, he got out and moved to California. But there's still the concern he could show up again."

Ben remained silent for several minutes. Then he said, "Look, man, I know that was a horrible ordeal, but it wasn't your fault. It could have happened to anyone."

Cam turned guilty eyes to him. "Of course it was my fault. I was texting instead of watching Finn."

"Come on, man, everyone gets distracted now and then."

Cam shook his head again. "I'll still never forgive myself. And if Finn hadn't been found unharmed, I don't know what I would have done."

"You're human, Cam. Every single one of us makes mistakes."

Cam nodded. "Exactly. And I don't want to make another one."

Ben's eyebrows drew together. "I don't understand."

A deep sigh hissed through Cam's lips. "Brian. I can't take the chance that I might do something to endanger him."

Ben stared at him, wide-eyed. "Buddy, that's just plain crazy. You can't go through life worrying about things that may never happen."

"And nothing will happen to Brian because of me if I'm not around." Cam leveled his gaze back at Ben.

Ben shook his head. "Do you realize how ridiculous that sounds? It's like never going swimming because you're afraid you'll drown. Or never riding a horse because you're afraid you'll be bucked off. Or never driving a car because—"

"I get the picture."

"The point is, buddy, you need to let this go and stop living in fear."

Cam blew out a frustrated breath. "I can't. It's always with me."

"Then maybe you need to see a counselor. This mindset isn't healthy."

Cam snorted. "A shrink? So now I'm nuts?"

Ben lowered his gaze. "Look. You love Olivia, right?"

Without answering aloud, Cam hesitated, then nodded.

"And don't you think she's going to need help raising her nephew?"

Cam held up his hands. "I can't help her—"

Ben compressed his lips. "Then you need to let her know why. It isn't fair to her to just walk out on her with no explanation."

"You're right." Cam gathered the reins in his left hand and stuck his foot in Kimber's left stirrup. "Thanks for listening." He rode off before Ben could respond.

Now he had more confusing thoughts to digest. Ben was right about one thing. Cam did owe Olivia an explanation. But how was he going to explain while, at the same time, letting her know he couldn't risk hurting

Brian? And how was he going to live his life alone again?

175

Chapter Twenty-Five

Olivia sat at the large oak table in Darcy's massive kitchen sipping iced tea. She had kept the tears to a minimum this time as she related the strangest breakup she'd ever experienced. Darcy, in turn, had filled her in on what Cam had shared with Ben. Olivia mulled over everything Darcy said.

"Granted, it was a terrible experience but isn't Cam taking the kidnapping to an extreme, letting it control his life?" Olivia stirred sugar into her second glass of tea.

"It still haunts him." Darcy squeezed lemon into her own glass. She picked up another lemon wedge, sucked out the juice, puckered her cheeks, and set the rind on her napkin.

Olivia sighed. "I knew things were too good to be true." She shook her head. "But that's it for me. No more men in my life." She stopped and smiled. "Except for Brian, of course."

"How is Brian adjusting?" Darcy plucked a sugar cookie from the plate before them and nibbled around the edges.

"Oh, he's doing great." Olivia warmed to the new

subject, one she would never tire of. "He started preschool on Monday, and you won't believe how smart he is."

Darcy smiled, encouraging her to go on.

"He already knows all his letters and his phonics. He'll be reading in no time."

"It sounds like you were born for this."

Olivia laughed. "A few months ago, if you'd told me I'd be the mother of a four-year-old, I would have said you were crazy. But honestly, Darcy, I can't imagine how I lived without him."

Mac barked to be let into the kitchen, and Darcy rose to open the door. "And the adoption? How's that going?"

The dog immediately ran to Olivia's side, his whole rear end wagging, waiting to be petted. Olivia obliged. "It's in the process. We just have to wait for things to be finalized." She took a sip of her tea. "Even Mom is excited. She says she's finally going to be a grandmother. Who would have thought? But Brian stole her heart like he stole mine. Oh! I forgot to tell you. We found a new apartment."

"That's great. Where?" Darcy looked at Mac, who now had his front feet in Olivia's lap. "Mac! Down!"

"He's okay."

Darcy raised her eyebrows. "He's learning bad manners."

"Fine. Sorry, Mac." Olivia shoved his feet off the chair. "It's actually much closer to here, on the near side of town. It has two bedrooms, one-and-a-half baths, and a much bigger kitchen." She laughed. "I guess I'm going to have to learn how to cook." At her admission, a shard of pain pierced her heart. Cam had told her he could cook, which had been his odd way of almost proposing. Well, he wasn't going to be around, so she'd better suck it up and make sure she and Brian didn't starve. "We can move in this weekend."

"Great. I'll ask the guys to bring their trucks and help."

Olivia bit her lip. "Well, I could use Ben and Ricky's help."

~

On Saturday, all three men showed up with their pickups. Olivia's heart fluttered at Cam's presence, but she tried to keep things as impersonal and detached as possible. At one point, Cam touched her arm and asked if he could speak to her.

Her eyes traveled to the parking lot where everyone else loaded the trucks. She looked at Cam and nodded, leading him to her small kitchen. Leaning against the sink, she crossed her arms and waited for him to begin.

"Olivia, I owe you an apology and an explanation," he said.

"I already know."

His brows drew together. "Know what?"

"About what happened to your nephew. About the kidnapping."

He blew out a breath. "Oh." He swiped a hand across his face. "I'm sorry, Olivia, I should have told you. I *meant* to tell you—"

"Do you think it would have made any difference to me? That I would have thought differently about you?" She willed herself not to cry.

"No, but . . . I can't . . ."

"You're afraid that something like that might

happen again if you're with Brian."

He nodded, averting his eyes.

"Well, Cam, I'm sorry for you." As he raised astonished eyes back to hers, she continued. "Because you are living in fear, you'll never know the joy of being around an amazing little boy who gives me nothing but happiness." She pushed past him and picked up a box, before turning once more to face him. "The Bible tells us that God does not want us to live in fear, but to have courage." She walked out the door, leaving him standing alone in the kitchen.

~

The words Olivia had spoken to him played over and over in Cam's mind. He knew Scripture. He knew God didn't want His people living in fear, yet Cam couldn't shake the visceral response that paralyzed him every time he thought of what had happened to Finn. It wasn't just that Finn had been kidnapped—it was the fact that Cam had been responsible. He also knew God had forgiven him, even if Annette hadn't. Even if he hadn't forgiven himself. So why couldn't he move on? Should he seek therapy from a counselor? But who? He'd never been in a position to need services of this kind. He'd always been strong, capable of handling his own problems, able to push through whatever he needed to do to get the job done. But clearly, he wasn't pushing through this part of his past that held him hostage. Still, what could a counselor do? A counselor couldn't change what had happened. And besides, even if Cam ever did learn to come to terms with the damage he had caused, he'd lost Olivia forever.

Chapter Twenty-Six

The days turned into weeks, and Olivia and Brian settled into a comfortable rhythm. She had taken him to the ranch a few times, and he had been thrilled with the horses. She even learned to cook some simple meals, and her mother helped on the nights she worked. September rolled around bringing a chill to the air and brilliant colors to the trees.

One Saturday, Olivia bundled Brian in his jacket and said, "We're going on an adventure today."

Brian's eyes twinkled in excitement, and she chuckled. Everything for Brian was new and exciting, and she loved introducing him to new experiences and seeing things for the first time through his child's eyes. "Where, Mommy?"

Her heart sang. After the adoption was finalized, Brian had started calling her 'Mommy,' and Olivia had never heard such a sweet word. She touched his nose. "You'll see."

She buckled him into his car seat and drove to the edge of town to the park where she and Cam had hiked to the beautiful overlook. That outing seemed so long ago. She sat for a moment after turning off the engine, praying silently to shed the sadness that had cocooned her like a heavy cloak when she pulled into the parking area. This was supposed to be a fun outing with Brian. Although she sensed no immediate peace, she forced herself to open her car door and get out. She took in a bracing breath of chilly air and removed Brian from his car seat.

"Do you want to see something special?" she asked.

"Yeah!" came his enthusiastic answer.

"It's a long walk. Uphill. Can you do that?"

"I can, Mommy, watch." He took off into the woods laughing, his feet crunching the dried leaves.

"Slow down. Wait for me." She followed, not quite as quickly. Brian ran ahead, stopping every few feet to wait for her. He struggled a little when the trail steepened, but he persevered. When they reached the "snake" rock, as she had come to think of it, she skirted a wide path around it, although she knew her reaction was silly. It wasn't as though the snake lay in wait for her. Besides, snakes usually didn't venture out in cold weather.

Brian's energy began to falter, and Olivia suggested a piggyback ride. Moving her backpack to her front, she squatted and allowed him to climb onto her back. Continuing up the trail with his added weight slowed her progress but they finally emerged at the overlook.

"We're here, Brian," she said, easing him to his feet.

"Wow," he said, his voice hushed in awe.

The fall foliage added magnificent splashes of color to the already glorious landscape. "It's even more beautiful than the last time I was here." She patted the flat ledge. "Come, let's sit and enjoy this amazing picture God painted for us."

"God painted this?" he asked, his eyes wide.

She giggled. She would have to remember how literally four-year-olds took everything. "In a manner of speaking, yes. Are you hungry? I thought this would be a good place for a picnic."

He smiled in answer, and she opened her backpack to dig out the sandwiches and cookies she had packed. As they ate their lunch, Olivia couldn't help but reflect on the last time she'd been here with Cam. He'd promised to bring her back in the fall. So much for his promise. For a fleeting moment, she allowed herself to imagine how wonderful it would be if all three of them could be enjoying this day together. But dwelling on that fantasy would do no good. Her life wasn't going to suddenly change into happily ever after.

The chill of sitting on the cold rock worked its way into her bones, and she shivered. She noticed Brian's eyelids becoming heavy and his head starting to nod against his chest.

Getting to her feet, she brushed off the seat of her pants and said, "Time to head back. Are you too sleepy to walk?"

Brian popped up like a cork. "I'm not sleepy, Mommy. I can walk."

She grinned and readjusted his cap over his cold-reddened ears. "If you get too tired, let me know and I'll give you another piggyback ride." Secretly, she hoped he could make the climb back down, as going down the steep trail with him on her back could be precarious. She remembered falling the last time. If only Cam were here, he could carry the child—*Stop*! Why was Cam suddenly all over her thoughts? Well, of course, this place reminded her of the time they'd spent here, that wonderful, perfect day. Maybe coming here hadn't been such a good idea. No, she wouldn't allow herself to think that way. *She'd* promised to come here in the fall, and she kept promises to herself. Besides, she'd enjoyed this special outing with Brian.

Olivia descended first, reaching out her hand to help Brian climb down. He giggled and jumped around, making the adventure much more fun, pointing out leaves and insects and plants. Even when she saw signs of him tiring, he valiantly kept up, never complaining or asking to be carried.

When they reached the parking lot, he said, "That was fun, Mommy. Can we come here again tomorrow?"

Her legs answered with a protest, and she let out a loud groan. "I don't think my old body can make that climb again so soon."

"You're not old," he said. "My other mommy was old. She couldn't run and play with me like you do."

Sadness pierced Olivia's heart. She knelt and took hold of Brian's arms. "Sweetie, that wasn't because your real mommy was old. It was because she was sick. She couldn't help it. She couldn't be as strong as she wanted to be. Do you understand?"

His face grew solemn. "I know. I miss my other mommy." Tears welled up in his big brown eyes.

He hadn't talked much about Martha, and Olivia didn't know whether that was a good thing or a bad thing. She pulled him against her shoulder, her own tears stinging the backs of her eyes. "I know you do, sweetie. I do, too. But she loved you very much."

He sniffled and pulled away, wiping his nose on his sleeve.

"And I love you very much, too. You're a lucky boy to have two mommies who love you. One in Heaven and one here on Earth."

He seemed to consider her words, then he smiled. "Yeah."

~

Cam had been seeing Dr. Mercer for several weeks. At first, he'd been somewhat embarrassed to discuss his personal business with a complete stranger, especially the fear he hadn't shared with anyone until recently. Cam was not a touchy-feely guy, and talking about his feelings did not come easily for him. But Dr. Mercer allowed him to take his time, revealing bits and pieces of his heart a little at a time. He had been understanding, rather than dismissive, and assured Cam that his anxiety was normal after the ordeal he had been through. But he expressed his concern that he didn't want Cam to be held captive to that fear for the rest of his life, and Cam finally acknowledged that he didn't either.

He was slowly learning techniques to help him cope with his panic attacks. Of course, not being around Brian made the whole process easier. But he missed Olivia so much it sometimes hurt to breathe. Dr. Mercer encouraged him to reach out to her, but Cam knew it was too late. He was cordial to her when their paths crossed at the ranch, but he didn't take steps to try to rebuild their relationship. He had burned that bridge.

Chapter Twenty-Seven

Cam held the phone and let out a whoop. "You're kidding! You're really coming to visit me?"

His father's deep chuckle rumbled through the phone. "Well, we can't get you to come home, so your mother insisted I take a long weekend and drive down to see you."

"That's great news, Dad. When?"

"This weekend. We'll come down Friday and leave Monday morning. We want to see this ranch of yours."

Cam snorted. "It's not *my* ranch, Dad. But it's beautiful. You'll love it."

"I'm sure we will. But if you want the honest truth, I think what your mother really wants is to see this girl you've been dating. Your mom's tired of waiting for you to bring her for a visit."

"Oh." Cam's smile disappeared. "About that. Uh, we're not exactly together anymore."

His father didn't comment for a minute. "Son, I'm sorry to hear that. It sounded like you really cared about her."

I did. Cam cleared his throat. "If you don't want

to come—"

"No, of course we still want to come." Dad's cheerful tone sounded a bit forced. "Oh, and I almost forgot. Guess who's coming with us?"

Cam held his breath. Not Annette and Finn! But who else would they be bringing? "Annette?" His voice raised on a note of hope.

"Your sister says she misses you and wants to see you. You won't believe how much Finn's grown since you saw him last."

Annette. He'd almost given up on her ever wanting to be a part of his life again. But Finn! Cam's heart stuttered before he took in several deep breaths and released them slowly. He wouldn't be expected to watch out for Finn. He knew Annette would never let him out of her sight.

"Son, you there?"

Cam swallowed. "Yeah, I'm here, Dad. I can't wait to see you."

~

Cam's face stretched into a huge grin when he saw his dad's truck pull into the parking space behind his. He raced down the steps of his apartment complex and wrapped his mother in a bear hug the minute she stepped out of the vehicle.

"Man, it's good to see you," he breathed against her neck. When had his mom gotten so small? He realized it had been a while since he'd seen his family, and he vowed he would never let so much time go by again without going home.

His father circled to the passenger side of the truck and slapped Cam on the back as he released his mother. "You look good, son. I'm glad we finally decided to come see where you live." He pulled Cam into a man hug.

"It's about time." Cam chuckled.

Annette exited more slowly, standing a few feet away, eyeing him warily. Finn piled out behind her, and she slung a protective arm around his shoulders.

"Sis, thank you for coming." Cam stepped to her and gave her an awkward hug. He felt her stiffen under his embrace. Suppressing a sigh, he looked down at Finn and stuck out his hand. "Hey, buddy. It's been a long time since I've seen you. Look how big you are."

Finn returned the handshake in a masculine manner, then blurted out, "Are you really a cowboy, Uncle Cam?" His eyes widened with admiration.

"I really am, Finn, but the job isn't nearly as glamorous as you might think."

"Finn is quite impressed with the cowboys at your uncle's ranch," said his mother. "He can't believe his very own uncle is a cowboy, too. You're a folk hero in his eyes."

"Well, how about tomorrow morning I take you out to Whispering Winds Ranch where I work?

"Yeah! That'd be great, Uncle Cam." Finn looked at his mother, his eyes dancing with excitement.

"For now, we'd better get over to the hotel and unload our bags. Then we're taking you out to dinner," said Dad.

"Why don't I follow you, then we can go straight to the restaurant?"

"Can I ride with you, Uncle Cam? Please?"

Cam hesitated, his eyes traveling to Annette's. The corners of her mouth turned up ever so slightly. "Yes, I suppose so. But don't talk your uncle's ear off."

"Yes!" Finn punched the air with his fist, then scampered into the cab of Cam's truck.

Contrary to his mother's admonition, Finn chattered nonstop all the way to the hotel, then all the way to the restaurant. Cam found his nephew just as delightful as he'd been three years earlier, and it seemed as though their relationship had simply picked up where it left off. The long separation hadn't dampened their relationship at all, which seemed incredible as Finn had not quite turned three years old when Cam left. Even more importantly, Cam wasn't nervous being alone with Finn, even if they were just riding in his truck. They ate at a local pizza parlor—Finn's suggestion—then headed back to Cam's apartment.

Everybody talked at once, catching up, and Cam basked in the warmth he had missed from being with his family. Finally, Finn's energy turned off like a switch, and he fell asleep leaning against Cam.

"It's late," said Dad, rising from his seat. "We'd better head back and get this little cowboy into bed." He reached for his grandson who didn't even stir as he lifted him from the couch.

Mom stood, too, but Annette held back. "Do you two mind taking Finn and putting him to bed? I'd like to stay and talk with Cam for a little while."

His parents exchanged looks, then his mother said, "Of course not, but how will you get back to the hotel?"

"I can drive her back," said Cam.

"Well, all right. We'll see you in the morning." His mother gave him a peck on the cheek and his father gave him another pat on the back.

"I'll make breakfast. Come by around eight," said Cam. *I can cook.* The thought from out of nowhere blindsided him and for a brief second, his heart sat like dead weight in his chest. He shook off the memory and relegated it to a corner of his brain reserved for "later."

Cam closed the door behind his parents, Finn still asleep on Dad's shoulder, and turned to Annette. She sat on the edge of her seat, her hands twisting in her lap.

"Would you like more to drink?" he asked, nodding to her empty water glass.

She shook her head and bit her lip, as he waited for her to say whatever she couldn't say in front of the others.

Cam settled back on the sofa, his left ankle crossed over his right knee, and studied his younger sister. She looked older—older than her true age. Worry lines were etched between her brows and around her eyes. He knew the years had been hard on her, first with her marriage and divorce, then being a single parent. Her dark hair had flecks of gray here and there, and her eyes held a lifetime of sorrow.

"Cam, I want to tell you how sorry I am for the way I've treated you," she said, raising tear-filled eyes to his.

"No, Annie, it was my fault—" He couldn't remember the last time he'd used his pet name for his sister.

She shook her head with more vehemence, cutting him off. "No, Cam, if anything it was *my* fault. I knew what Joel was capable of and I should have warned you." She swiped her index finger under her eyes, catching escaping tears.

Cam rose and retrieved a box of tissues from the

bathroom, thrusting them into her hand.

"I blamed you because I knew the same thing could have just as easily happened to me, and I couldn't bear that thought." She plucked a tissue from the box and dabbed her eyes.

His brows drew together in confusion. "Annie, I don't understand."

"What happened was an accident. Do you know how many times I've gotten distracted and lost track of Finn?"

"But—"

She held up a restraining hand. "No, Cam, I've harbored misplaced bitterness toward you for way too long, and it's poisoning me. You're not the bad guy here. You've suffered just as much as I have—maybe more."

He swallowed hard, willing the lump in his throat to dislodge.

"I've been unreasonable. And . . . and cruel to keep punishing you." Her voice broke on a sob. "I've missed you so much." She bent forward, her face in her hands, and gave way to noisy weeping.

Cam crossed the short distance between them, knelt in front of her, and rocked her against his shoulder. "It's all right."

"Can you forgive me? I know I can't take back all the ugly things I said—"

"You're forgiven. Do you forgive me?"

She pulled back and drew in a long, shaky breath. "Of course."

He smiled and blinked away his own tears. "You don't know how happy you've made me."

She smiled back and blew her nose. "I love you,

Cam. I'm sorry it's taken me so long to reconcile with you."

"Better late than never."

A sad laugh erupted from her lips.

"I love you, too, Annie," he said softly.

After one final wipe of her nose, she crumpled the tissue and said, "I want you to be a part of Finn's life. He idolizes you, Cam, even though you haven't been around. You're like the family legend."

"That's a lot of expectation to live up to." Cam ran a hand through his hair, thinking about the responsibility of being someone's idol. "Perhaps I can be a male role model rather than an idol." Surprisingly, the idea didn't frighten him. It actually sounded rather nice.

"I'm seeing someone," she said, abruptly changing the subject. A sly smile appeared on her face.

"That's what Mom said. Is it serious?"

She nodded. "Yes, I think so. But I'm taking things slowly."

"That's smart. Does Finn like him?"

"Yes, very much. And he adores Finn."

"I'm happy for you, Annie. When do I get to meet this man and give my approval? You do know he has to pass my inspection."

A blush crept into her already tear-reddened cheeks. "Soon, I hope." Then her expression saddened. "Mom told me about your special lady. Any chance—"

"No, I blew it." Cam turned away, not wanting to discuss Olivia.

Annette put a hand on his arm. "I'm sorry, Cam."

Grateful that his sister intuitively sensed he didn't want to discuss his failed relationship, he said, "I'd better get you back to the hotel. Mom and Dad will be thinking we're out being wild and crazy."

She laughed. "I'll bet that's not easy in this little town."

"You have no idea." He rose and handed her her jacket before reaching for his own.

"Do you want me to help with breakfast in the morning?"

"Nope. I've got it covered. Believe it or not, I'm a good cook." The words stung him again as he opened the door for her and followed her out into the chilly night.

Chapter Twenty-Eight

"Can we go to the ranch today and see the kittens?" Brian bounced in his breakfast seat, his cereal more on the table than in his bowl.

Olivia paused. "Oh, Brian, I don't know. I don't have to work today and I wanted to—"

"Please? I haven't seen them in a long, long time."

She grinned. He hadn't seen the kittens for a week. But to a four-year-old, a week could be an eternity. Besides, the kittens were changing so quickly, and at four weeks old, they were starting to develop their individual personalities.

A stray cat had shown up at the barn a few weeks earlier, as stray cats were prone to do. This one, however, was pregnant. Brian had been following the progress of the kittens from the time they were just a couple of days old, and Olivia had promised him when the kittens were big enough, he could pick out one to bring home.

"All right," she agreed. "But just for a few minutes. We've got a lot of errands to run."

"Yay!" He jumped up from the breakfast table.

"I'll get my shoes."

"Wait, your breakfast," she called after him, but she knew he wouldn't settle down long enough to finish. Sighing, she carried his bowl to the sink and rinsed it, placing it in the dishwasher. Then she wiped up the mess at his place. A half-drunk glass of chocolate milk remained, so she put it in the refrigerator for later.

Ten minutes later, they were in the car heading to the ranch. "Remember," she told him. "Just a few minutes."

"Can I choose my kitten today?"

"You can think about it, but they're still too little to bring home."

"I can't wait. I'm going to name him Tigger."

She smiled. The name had probably come from the Winnie-the-Pooh books he loved. "That's a fine name, Brian, but how do you know you'll choose a boy kitten?" She peeked in the rearview mirror to watch him mull over her question.

Finally, he shrugged and said, "I just do."

They pulled up to the ranch house, and Mac ran out barking a greeting.

"Can we get a dog, too, Mommy?" Brian sank to the ground and let Mac lick his face.

"Don't push your luck. One animal at a time." Spying Darcy's car, she said, "Brian, I need to tell Darcy something before we go to the barn. It'll just take a minute."

Olivia walked to the backdoor, rapped once, then pushed open the door and poked her head in. "Darcy? I need to let you know . . ." She stopped when she saw several people sitting around the large kitchen table, including Cam. "Oh, I'm sorry. I didn't realize you had company."

Darcy got up and ushered her in. "It's okay. These are Cam's parents, his sister, Annette, and nephew, Finn. Everyone, this is Olivia Anderson, our horseback riding instructor and trail leader."

Olivia's eyes darted around the table, and her discomfort level rose. She had no doubt they all knew her as more than Darcy's employee. Cam's parents stood and held out their hands. "It's nice to meet you, Mr. and Mrs. Ellis," she murmured.

"No, no, we're just Jim and Dorothy," said Cam's mother, hanging onto Olivia's hand in both of hers.

Cam's father indicated an empty chair next to him with a wave of his hand. "Won't you join us?"

"Oh, no, I . . . we—"

"Oh, come on, Olivia. We're just having a cup of coffee before Cam takes his family on a tour of the ranch. Besides, I need to talk to you." Darcy seemed to notice Brian for the first time. "Oh, and this is Olivia's son, Brian."

"We're going to see the kittens," Brian said.

"Kittens?" Finn looked at Cam.

"We have three kittens in the barn," said Cam. "They're four weeks old."

"Can I see them? Please?" He looked around the table at all the adults.

"Maybe in a little while," said Annette.

"Oh please, Mom? You're all just sitting here talking."

A gentle murmur of amusement went through the adults.

"I can show him," said Brian. "I know where they

are."

"Well—"

"Thanks, Mom. Come on, Brian." The two boys dashed out the door faster than anyone could react.

"I guess our talk is pretty boring to a six-year-old," said Dorothy. "But I need this second cup of coffee to fortify me before traipsing around this huge ranch."

"Have a seat, Olivia," Darcy urged again.

Trapped, Olivia sat next to Jim. Cam poured a cup of coffee and passed it to her along with the cream and sugar, making her feel even more uneasy. How well he knew her tastes.

"So, tell us about yourself and Brian," said Dorothy, and all eyes turned to Olivia.

Olivia took a sip of coffee, wondering how long she'd have to stay in this awkward situation until she could gracefully make an exit. They had to know the history between her and their son. Did they think of her as a heartbreaker? Or a tease? Or worse? She tried to keep her answer short. "I adopted my sister's son, Brian, after she died."

"Oh my," said Dorothy, sympathy coloring her tone. "That must have been so difficult for you." She continued to ask question after question, listening with a genuine interest.

Olivia found herself talking about Martha and their family issues, and how they'd been separated for several years before Martha had made contact with her again, and how she'd ended up with Brian. As she related her story, she noticed all of them watching her thoughtfully, their full attention directed to her words.

"What a wonderful thing to do," said Dorothy.

"Not everyone would be willing to take on the responsibility of raising a small child."

For the first time since she'd sat down, Olivia relaxed in the presence of Cam's welcoming family. "To be honest, Brian is the best thing that's ever happened to me," she said, deliberately avoiding looking at Cam. "I can't imagine my life without him."

"That little boy certainly livens things up around here," said Darcy.

Olivia felt drawn to these warm people and began asking about their lives. Annette filled her in on her job as a receptionist for a doctor's office, and she talked with pride about her son. Cam's parents told several funny stories, some relating to Cam. Despite herself, she couldn't help but glance in Cam's direction and grin when his family shared embarrassing incidents from his childhood.

Finally, Cam said, "Enough," and looked at his watch. "If we don't get a move on, the day will be shot."

"Gracious, I didn't realize how long we've been sitting here," said Dorothy. "As much as I've enjoyed talking, I really want to see your beautiful ranch, Darcy."

Annette frowned. "The boys have sure been gone a long time."

The same thought ran through Olivia's mind. "They're probably absorbed in playing with the kittens. I'll go round them up."

"I'll go with you," said Annette. "I'd love to see the kittens."

Olivia laughed. "Careful, or you'll be taking one home with you."

The two women walked to the barn, chatting away as if they'd known each other all their lives. Olivia couldn't imagine a more wonderful, close-knit family, and she wondered about the rift between Cam and his sister. There didn't appear to be any tension between them today, as far as Olivia could tell.

"Olivia, may I ask you something that's none of my business?"

Olivia sighed. She knew what was coming. "You want to know what happened between Cam and me."

Annette smiled. "Am I that obvious?" When Olivia raised her eyebrows at the question, Annette continued. "Well, I realize I've only known you for a very short time, but it seems to me you're perfect for each other."

"Thank you, that means a lot." Olivia stopped just short of the barn and lowered her voice, not wanting the boys to overhear. "The fact is he couldn't handle Brian."

"What do you mean? He seems like such a sweet little boy."

"He is, but Cam is still traumatized by what happened with Finn. He can't face the possibility of anything happening to another child in his care."

"What?" Annette's face drained of color. "Oh my word, I had no idea." Tears sprang to her eyes. "And I made things worse by blaming him. By saying terrible things to him."

Olivia touched her arm. "It's nobody's fault. It was a horrible nightmare for all of you."

"But to cripple Cam to the point where he is afraid to be around children . . ." Her voice broke.

"It's okay, Annette. Cam and I just weren't meant

to be, that's all." She started walking toward the barn again. "Come on, let's see those kittens. That'll cheer you up." They entered the barn, and Olivia called out, "Boys?"

She headed to the back corner where the mother cat had made her nest. The cat lay nursing her kittens, but there was no sign of the boys. "Hmm, that's funny. I wonder where they are." She turned 360 degrees scanning the interior of the dimly-lit barn. "Brian? Finn?"

When no answer came, she said, "They must have gotten bored and wandered out to the paddock to see the horses."

Annette followed her out to the paddock where several horses raised their heads to greet Olivia and inspect the newcomer. A couple of horses came over to the fence, and Olivia gave them a half-hearted pat as her eyes searched the perimeter for the boys.

"I can't imagine where they would have gone," she said more to herself than to Annette. She raised her voice and called their names again.

"What's going on?" asked Jim. The adults had finally come out of the house and wandered down to the paddock.

"We can't find the boys," said Olivia, a twinge of concern lodging in her gut.

"They have to be around here somewhere," said Dorothy.

All the adults called repeatedly, but no answer came.

"Think, Olivia," said Darcy. "Where else did Brian like to go on the ranch?"

Olivia closed her eyes and pinched the bridge of

her nose, trying to focus her thoughts. "Nowhere, we're always close to the barn or the . . . Oh, no!" Her eyes flew open and her heart began to pound. "The creek. Last week I took him to the creek. But it's way too far for them to have walked to. Don't you think?" She turned questioning eyes on Darcy, hoping her friend would dismiss her rising fear.

A shadow crossed Darcy's face. "I don't know, but with all the rain we've have this past week, the creek is really up. It was overflowing the banks yesterday."

Olivia's rising fear gave way to full-blown panic. In the few seconds it took her to process the implications of the boys possibly being at the creek, Ben rode up, his morning rounds completed.

"I need the horse!" shouted Cam. He practically pulled Ben out of the saddle and climbed up, spurring the animal into a gallop.

Olivia's racing heart threatened to burst through her chest as she tried to compose herself enough to form a coherent plan. "I'm going, too," she cried, quickly unlatching the gate and hoisting herself atop Windsong, riding bareback away from the paddock.

Chapter Twenty-Nine

Cam kept up a silent plea to the rhythm of Dandy's hoofbeats. "Please, God, please, God, please, God." He remembered uttering those same two words over and over when Finn had been abducted, and déjà vu smacked into him with a fury. He couldn't bear it if something happened to those boys. Worse yet, he knew Annette and Olivia would never recover. Cam leaned forward in the saddle, urging the horse to go faster, as Dandy thundered across the grassy, tree-lined expanse leading to the creek. In the depths of his soul, Cam knew that's where the boys had gone.

What if he was too late? They had lost track of time while they sat around the kitchen table talking, and now he mentally flogged himself for not paying closer attention. His heart drummed with urgency, his mind consumed with reaching the water, as the chilly wind whipped through his hair. Finally, he heard the sound of the burbling brook in the distance. But no children's voices. Fear held him in a fierce grip, and Cam took several deep breaths to restore calm. It would do nobody any good if he fell apart now.

As he neared the bank of the creek through a

clearing of trees, he yelled, "Finn! Brian!" He dismounted before bringing Dandy to a complete stop and ran toward the shore. Did he hear something? He paused for a moment, searching the rapidly flowing water, and called again. It might have been only the wind playing tricks on him, but he swore he'd heard a voice. He quickly pulled off his boots and waded into the icy water, his wet jeans clinging to his legs. From the center of the stream, he scanned both shores of the creek bed, the swift-moving current nearly pulling him downstream.

There! He heard it again. Faint, but definitely a voice. He gave himself up to the current, allowing it to move him along as he swam with powerful strokes, carefully avoiding fallen logs and floating debris. The water flowed around a bend, and there at the crook, he spied a patch of color. Finn and Brian were caught in some low-hanging branches, their panicked movements to escape only trapping them more. The high water intermittently rushed over their heads as they struggled to free themselves.

"Don't move!" Cam shouted. "I'm coming." He fought the force of the water trying to pull him further downstream from the boys as he slogged his way toward the branches, feeling like his legs were mired in quicksand.

At last, he reached the tangle of vegetation and searched for a purchase to keep himself from being swept away. He grabbed hold of a sturdy-looking limb and pulled the boys from the ensnarement, pushing them toward the surface. Their heads bobbed out of the water, and they came up coughing and spitting water. Brian began to cry.

"It's okay, I've got you, buddy," said Cam. Brian wrapped his arms around Cam's neck, threatening to pull him under. Cam nudged Finn against a branch. "Hand on tight for just another minute."

"Cam? Brian? Finn?" Olivia's voice rang out through the copse of trees at the water's edge.

"In here," he yelled back. "I've got them. Come straight through the trees toward my voice."

He heard the rustling of leaves and snapping of twigs as she ran through the dense overgrown thicket, finally emerging at the side of the stream.

"Take Brian," he yelled, trying to move closer to the edge. "Be careful, don't fall in."

Olivia looked around and grabbed onto a large root sticking out of the ground a few feet away from where the boys were trapped. Her feet slid down the muddy embankment, and she dangled with one hand clinging to the root, the other reaching out to brace herself. Cam moved laterally, inching along, fighting the current, until he narrowed the gap between them.

She stretched out her arm. "Grab my hand, Brian," she yelled.

Brian initially refused to let go of his death grip on Cam's neck, but Cam gently pried his arms away, pushing him toward Olivia.

"Come on, Brian, just a little further," she coaxed. She leaned forward, straining to reach the child.

With a great heave, Cam thrust Brian forward, and Olivia latched onto his hand. She pulled him up onto the bank and collapsed into the mud, Brian's arms now in a death grip around *her* neck.

Cam turned back to Finn. "Hang on, buddy, I'm coming." He trudged back to where he had left Finn, his movements clumsy against the swirling water.

"Hurry, Uncle Cam, my hands are slipping! I can't hold on!" The current repeatedly crashed against Finn's body, forcing him up against the fragile mesh of thin branches and leaves dangling in the water and tearing at his grip.

Cam fought against the downward pull of the stream as he worked his way to the middle of the creek. Just as he reached out his hand to grab his nephew, the strong flowing water wrenched Finn from his flimsy security and dragged him away in the churning current.

"No!" screamed Cam. He watched helplessly as his nephew was swept further downstream, his body tossed about as though it weighed no more than a leaf. The child fought to keep his head above water, but the swirling waves spun and washed over him mercilessly as they rushed toward their end.

Cam plunged after him, bumping up against submerged rocks and branches as he swam with every ounce of strength he could muster. He could still see Finn up ahead, but it seemed as though the distance between them grew longer. His heavy, water-soaked jeans were slowing him down. He took a few precious seconds to unzip his jeans and tug them off, freeing his legs. Once unencumbered, he made up for lost time, gradually narrowing the space, but he found his strength starting to weaken the longer he remained in the icy water.

"Please, God," he gasped, his breathing rapid and shallow. "If I never do anything else in my life, let me do this one thing. Let me save Finn."

Finn does not belong to you. He belongs to me. He always has.

The words pummeled Cam's heart like a heavy fist, and at first, too stunned to respond, he stopped struggling and merely allowed himself to float. The words both encouraged and frightened him. Was God telling him Finn was going to die?

"If you take Finn, then take me, too," Cam prayed.

I am with you.

A strange peace settled over him like a protective blanket. Cam realized his body no longer shivered with the cold. Still not sure what to make of the strange message, he began to move with more deliberate strokes through the chaotic water. The creek made another turn, and Cam lost sight of Finn. Adrenaline—or something much more powerful—fueled him forward until he rounded the bend and spied Finn once again caught in a web of overhanging branches. Relief flooded through him until he noticed that Finn's head hung down and his body dangled limply against its trap.

"No, God, please!" Cam pushed through the remaining few yards until the water swept him against his nephew's body. "Finn!" Cam's agonizing cry carried above the roar of the water. With superhuman strength, he grasped his nephew and pulled him toward the bank. Then he lifted him out of the stream, struggling to climb the muddy embankment. With each step forward, he slid backward. Gritting his teeth, he slung Finn over his shoulder and grasped for whatever he could to pull himself up, slowly gaining traction.

Once on level ground, he laid Finn on the muddy terrain and quickly examined his inert body for signs of breathing. The blue tint to the child's lips made his heart skip a beat, but he pressed his fingers to Finn's neck, erupting with a shout of joy at finding a pulse. He placed his mouth against Finn's and blew two short breaths, watching as the boy's chest rose.

On the third breath, Finn coughed and then retched, releasing a good amount of water from his stomach. He took a few shaky breaths and then began to shiver violently. Cam picked him up, clutching him to his own body—although he was no warmer than Finn—and walked on unsteady legs through the few yards of trees leading to the grassy field beyond. There, he fell to the ground and covered Finn's frigid body with his.

It seemed like forever until help arrived, but finally he found himself surrounded by his parents, Annette, Ben and Darcy, and Olivia, holding Brian who was wrapped in a blanket. Cam sat up, his teeth chattering, and his mother placed a heavy quilt around him, then knelt and sobbed against his shoulder. Annette gathered Finn into another blanket and sat on the grass holding him, sobbing, as well.

"Uncle C . . . C . . .Cam saved my life," said Finn, his voice quivering with cold.

"And Brian's life," said Olivia, tears coursing down her cheeks. "I don't know how to thank you." Her voice caught as she hugged Brian closer.

"Ricky's bringing the wagon," said Ben. "We'll get you loaded up and back to the house for a warm shower and something hot to drink."

Cam stood on rubbery legs and took in a deep breath. "Thank you, God," he whispered.

Annette struggled to her feet under the weight of her son, and leaned against Cam. "How can I ever repay you? I owe you everything," she said, her voice thick with tears.

Cam grinned. "You can buy me a new pair of jeans."

The tension suddenly lifted as laughter rippled through the group.

"Yeah, I wasn't going to say anything, but really, buddy, aren't you a little old to be swimming in your underwear?" Ben slung an arm around Cam's shoulder and pulled him into a hug.

The rumble of the tractor sounded in the distance, and within a few minutes, Ricky appeared pulling the wagon behind him. Cam had never seen a more welcome sight. Well, except maybe for the boys. But now that his adrenaline rush had worn off, he felt drained and chilled to the bone. He climbed into the wagon and leaned back, closing his eyes.

Annette plopped down on one side of him and Olivia on the other. Both boys leaned into him, their wet heads pressed against his shoulder in complete trust of his protection. He freed his arms from the quilt and wrapped them around the boys, hugging them tighter, silent tears rolling down his face. Despite the tears, Cam had never felt so strong.

Chapter Thirty

After church the next day, the family gathered in Cam's apartment for lunch. With the crisis behind them, yet still very much on everyone's minds, they tried to restore things to a state of normalcy, which was difficult with Finn reliving every moment of his adventure.

"You really are his hero," said Annette. "Mine, too."

"Enough, already," said Cam. "It wasn't me. It was all the Lord."

"Be that as it may," said Mom, "the Lord used you as His vessel."

"Let's change the subject," said Dad, and Cam was more than ready to do so. "I've got something I want to talk with my son about."

His curiosity piqued, Cam turned his eyes to Dad. "This visit wasn't entirely just about seeing you and the ranch, which, by the way, we never finished seeing yesterday."

"Maybe we can go out today—"

Cam's father held up his hand. "No, that's not what I want to discuss with you." His father cleared his throat. "You know Uncle John's getting older, and running his ranch is starting to be too much for him."

Cam waited.

"You know he doesn't have any sons, and his daughters' husbands are not interested in ranching."

A glimmer of where this conversation might be headed dawned in Cam's mind.

His father ran his hand through his sparse, gray hair and continued. "Well, we were kind of wondering—your uncle and me—if you might be interested in coming back and taking over the ranch."

Cam's heart began to beat in a rapid tempo. It had always been his dream to stay at his uncle's ranch, perhaps one day take over, but the incident with Finn had changed everything. At that time, Annette had told him she never wanted to see him again and didn't want him around Finn, either. Cam knew her words came from a place of pain and terror, but he couldn't stay in the area, being a constant reminder of what she'd almost lost because of him.

He couldn't believe this was happening. A second chance to go home, do what he loved, and be with his family. "I . . . I don't know what to say."

"We hope you'll say yes," said Mom.

"Uncle John groomed you from the time you were Finn's age to one day take over for him," said Dad. "Eventually the ranch will belong to you."

The grin spreading across his face almost sprained his cheek muscles. "Wow. I never thought . . . after . . ."

Annette placed her hand on his arm. "That was my fault, Cam, and I'm so, so sorry. Would you please come home?"

He looked around the table, his eyes landing on

Finn. "On one condition. That Finn is my number one assistant."

Finn's eyes lit up. "You mean it, Uncle Cam?" He turned to his mother. "Mom, did you hear that? I'm going to be a cowboy just like Uncle Cam!"

Only one thing marred the joy of the moment. He would be leaving Olivia. And, much to his surprise, he found he would miss Brian, too.

~

Cam gave his notice the next day, and although Ben was sad to see him go, he was happy for the tremendous opportunity for Cam to manage his own ranch.

He sought out Olivia, waiting for her to finish her lesson. Then he quietly helped her untack the horses and put the equipment away, just like he used to do before he'd ruined everything between them. After they'd stored everything in the tack room, he hesitated, not knowing quite how to broach the subject.

"Well, thanks for helping me put everything away," Olivia said, obviously confused by his sudden helpfulness again. "I'd better go get Bri—"

"Olivia, I need to tell you something."

She paused just inside the doorway, waiting.

Cam blew out a breath and made himself meet her eyes. "I wanted to tell you before you heard it from someone else. I'm moving back home."

He saw her face crumple for just a fraction of a second before she regained her composure.

"I'm going to be taking over my uncle's ranch. You remember I told you about that."

She swallowed hard and nodded, then looked at her feet. "That's good," she said in a shaky voice. "I'm happy for you, Cam."

"I'll miss you. And Brian."

"We'll miss you, too." Her words came out in a whisper. "Um . . . thanks for telling me. I wish you all the best."

"You, too."

"I really need to go." She turned and fled.

He didn't go after her.

~

Olivia raced to her car, hoping Cam wouldn't follow. She couldn't bear for him to see the tears streaming down her face. She yanked open her car door and sat inside for a moment, noisy weeping erupting from her broken heart. She'd hoped that after Cam had heroically rescued the boys from the creek that he wouldn't be afraid of the uncertainties that came with raising children. They had all been at fault for not paying closer attention to the boys' whereabouts, and only Cam, after all, had managed to prevent a tragedy. Couldn't he see that unseen dangers were a part of life? He couldn't expect to keep loved ones safe twenty-four/seven. Still, she should be grateful for what he'd done for Brian, even if it didn't change the situation between them.

Pulling in a stuttering breath, she started her engine. She couldn't sit here crying. She had a son who was waiting for her at home.

Chapter Thirty-One

Cam rode Hannibal, his favorite horse, along the familiar hills and valleys of Uncle John's property, reacquainting himself with all the places he'd missed. How he loved this land. He surveyed the large herd of Black Angus cattle grazing in the pasture, their dark coats glistening under the weakening rays of the late fall sun contrasting with the browning grass. They ambled through the field, munching peacefully, the grinding of the grass in their molars like a soothing melody to Cam's cowboy ears. He took in a lungful of crisp, cold air and drank in the beauty of the surrounding landscape. Home. He was home.

He had never known such contentment, at least for the last few years. Being back with his family, his relationship with his sister and nephew restored, he couldn't ask for anything more. A sharp pang from out of nowhere poked at his heart, and he knew it was the hole left by Olivia. He'd tried to put her out of his mind, but he supposed that wound would always be with him, like tender scar tissue. Still, Olivia was in his past. He couldn't fix the irreparable mess he'd made of that relationship. He hoped she found a good man someday. Funny how he kept thinking about Brian and how much he would enjoy teaching the boy about ranching. Brian, the sole reason he'd abandoned Olivia in the first place. Even though Olivia was more than grateful for his saving Brian's life, Cam couldn't possibly presume her feelings toward him went beyond gratitude. She wouldn't risk having her heart ripped out and stomped on again.

He sighed. Their brief relationship had been great while it lasted. Maybe, in time, he would meet another woman who could fill the void in his life, but it would be difficult to find one as perfect for him as Olivia. As he rode in solitude, the weight of regret pressed heavily upon him. He remembered the night they'd spent watching over Dandy after he colicked, and the memory of Olivia drooling in his lap as she slept brought a sad smile to his face. As did the image of her wobbling across the dance floor in her stilettos at the wedding. But the memory that slammed his gut the hardest was of the first time he'd kissed her under the stars. Somehow, he'd known her lips would be sweet and soft and warm. *Let her go*, he told himself. He'd disrupted her life enough.

The sound of approaching hoofbeats carried through the rising wind, and Cam smiled to see Uncle John riding toward him, his weathered face covered in a myriad of wrinkles. Despite his age, Uncle John still displayed strength and resilience. Cam's love for his generous uncle coursed through him, warming him in the face of the increasing, chilly wind.

Uncle John stopped his horse next to Cam and said, "Well, what do you think?"

Cam shook his head in pure awe. "It's just the

way I remembered. You've kept the ranch in amazing condition."

"Not without some blood, sweat, and tears. The aches and pains of managing this place are starting to affect me more and more every day." He shifted his weight in his saddle. "It's sure good to have you back."

"It's good to be back. I can't thank you enough, Uncle John."

His uncle grunted. "You're the one I should be thanking. With you on board, the ranch can stay in the family. It doesn't look like I'm going to have grandsons anytime soon, and maybe you can train that nephew of yours to follow in your footsteps."

Cam adjusted his hat to keep it from being blown away in the wind. "I think Finn will be an excellent protégé. He's got ranching in his blood."

"That he does. Come on back to the house. Ruth's got lunch almost ready."

Cam grinned. "If I have to eat too much of Aunt Ruth's cooking, I'll be too heavy to ride a horse."

Uncle John laughed. "You got that right. I found me a good woman when I snatched her up forty-five years ago. You need to find you a good woman, son. Makes all the difference in the world to go through life with the right woman by your side."

Cam's mind flashed to Olivia again, and his mood darkened. Forcing a smile, he said, "I'd offer to race you back to the house, but I don't want to show you up."

"Ha! I'm not dead yet, boy." Uncle John turned his horse and spurred it into a gallop, leaving Cam behind.

Cam waited a moment and then followed at a

slightly slower pace.

~

Staying busy helped keep Olivia's mind off Cam, but it was difficult when she half-expected to see him every time she went to work. Whispering Winds hadn't been the same since he left. Ben had hired another ranch hand, Mason, who expressed interest in her, but she had no desire for anything more than a professional relationship, even if he did have Hollywood good looks.

Darcy had not pushed her to talk, for which Olivia was grateful. But one evening, when it was just the two of them, Darcy asked, "How are you holding up?"

Olivia paused, averting her eyes from her friend who tended to see too deeply into her soul. "I'm okay. Cam and I just weren't meant to be, that's all. It's probably best that he's gone."

Darcy sighed. "I'd hoped that after what happened with the boys, he would see things differently."

"I did, too," Olivia admitted. "But I can't change his feelings about children, and Brian comes first."

"You know," Darcy said, her words measured and slow, "Mason has been hovering around you like a bee."

Olivia barked out a mirthless laugh. "Don't go there. The last thing I need in my life right now is another man. Especially one I work with."

"Okay, I don't mean to intrude. It just hurts me to see you so down."

Olivia forced a smile. "I'll be fine. You're the vet. Time heals all wounds, right?"

Darcy hesitated. "Not all, I'm afraid."

~

"Cam?" A familiar voice rang out through the

cacophony of the cattle auction.

Cam stopped and turned. "Ben?" He pushed his way through the crowd toward his friend. The two men clapped each other on the shoulder and stood appraising the other. "Man, it's good to see you. I didn't know you were coming to this auction." Cam pulled Ben into a brief hug.

"It's the first time I've come this far north. I should have called to see if you would be here, but it didn't occur to me."

"Let's get out of this mob and find a quiet place to have a drink." Cam headed to the exit, Ben right behind him.

Once settled out of the way in a small café a few blocks from the market, the two men sipped large mugs of coffee and caught up.

"So, how is everything at your uncle's ranch? The North Star, isn't it?" Ben stirred more sugar into his cup.

"That's right. Things are good, really good. Uncle John has always maintained a top-rate place."

Ben tested the coffee with the added sweetness. "And how is your uncle's health?"

"He's doing well for his age, but I can see signs he's slowing down. The timing for me to come back couldn't have worked out better. How are things at Whispering Winds?"

Ben wiped his mouth with his napkin. "Going well. I hired a new hand named Mason. He's not as good as you, of course, but he shows promise."

Cam nodded. "I'm glad. I felt bad about leaving you short-handed, but the move back home seemed the right thing to do."

Ben waved his friend's comment aside. "Don't worry about it. You did what you needed to do for your family. God always provides, and He sent Mason."

Cam took a cautious sip of his hot coffee and debated asking the one question that floated in the air between them, the thought of which made his pulse spike.

Almost as though he read Cam's mind, Ben said, "Olivia and Brian are doing well."

Cam blinked a few times, then nodded again. "Good." He grinned. "That was quite an adventure those boys had on the creek, huh?"

Ben's expression was unreadable. "Yeah. You quite literally saved the day. That whole situation could have ended in tragedy if you hadn't acted so quickly."

Cam swallowed against his tight throat. "Sometimes I do something right."

"Don't be so modest." Ben hesitated. "Speaking of Olivia . . ."

Were they speaking of Olivia? Cam thought he had adeptly changed the subject. He took another sip of coffee and raised his eyes to Ben's, waiting.

"The new ranch hand, Mason, is quite taken with her."

A sucker punch landed in Cam's gut, and the Olivia-sized hole in his heart tore a little more. "Oh." He wrapped his hands around his mug to stop the trembling that had begun with Ben's news. Well, who could blame Mason for being taken with Olivia? Not only was she an excellent horsewoman, but her looks would cause any man to take notice.

"But she's not taken with him," Ben said pointedly.

Cam locked eyes with Ben. "Okay, buddy, what are you trying to tell me in a not-so-subtle roundabout way?"

Ben sighed and dropped his gaze. "Look, it may be none of my business, but I know when two people are right for each other."

Cam shook his head. "No, it's too late. I blew it."

"You're wrong. She still cares about you."

A spark of hope ignited in Cam's shattered heart. "How do you know? Did she tell you?"

"No, but I have eyes. She misses you something fierce."

Cam wanted to believe Ben, but he couldn't be so sure. "I don't know."

"You still care about her, right?" Ben lifted his gaze back to Cam again.

Cam nodded and mumbled, "Yeah, I do."

"Have you overcome your anxiety of being around children?"

Cam snorted. "Yeah, it's strange. I think about Brian all the time."

Ben reached across the table and gripped Cam's arm. "Then, buddy, you'd better make a move before Mason wears her defenses down."

Chapter Thirty-Two

Cam stewed over what Ben had said all the way home. He loved Olivia, he knew that much, despite his head trying to convince his heart otherwise. And he was fond of Brian, who, in time, he knew he could learn to love, as well. But did she really still have feelings for him? Would she give him a second chance? He knew he didn't deserve one. Was she already moving on to Mason? Even if Olivia did agree to give him another chance, would she be willing to uproot her life and move here? Was that fair to her? It would mean leaving her mother, her work, and her friends. It would mean uprooting Brian yet again after he finally had stability in his life. Was that fair to Brian?

His conflicting thoughts circled through his brain, leaving him frustrated and confused, and he arrived home emotionally drained. He dropped his duffel bag inside the door and stood for several minutes, his hands pressed to his temples. Suddenly, the need to hear her voice drowned out all the noise in his head. He had to talk to her, he had to know.

He glanced at his watch—11:20. Was it too late to call? Would he wake Brian? It didn't matter. He had to talk to her *now*. Before he lost his nerve, he fumbled for his phone, bringing up her contact information with a shaky hand, and punched in her number. She answered on the third ring, her voice thick with sleep.

"Hello? Cam? What's wrong?"

Now that he had her on the line, his nerve left him, and it took a few seconds to recover his courage.

"Cam? Are you there? Is everything okay?" Her voice rose with concern.

He closed his eyes and drew in a deep breath. "No, everything's not okay."

"What's wrong?" Her tone filled with alarm now, as she came fully awake.

"I miss you, Olivia. I love you." There, he had spit the words out. The next move was hers.

He heard a soft gasp on the other end. "Cam, what are you saying?"

A memory popped into his mind. He had used this tactic before, and it had almost worked. "I'm telling you I can cook. I'm actually a good cook."

Her sweet laughter reached his ear. "Seriously? Well, what if I told you I can cook now, too?"

"Oh." Deflated, he tried again. "Does this mean you don't need me?"

"Cam, what on earth? Why are you calling me out of the blue after all this time? What's going on?"

He sighed and rubbed a hand across his forehead. "Because I was a fool to let you go. I let my fears and insecurities get in the way of what mattered the most to me." His words rushed out faster than his brain could form them. "And after I came to terms with my challenges and was able to overcome them, I realized it was too late for us. I couldn't ask you to forgive me. I had hurt you too deeply. But I love you, Olivia, and I'm praying you will find it in your heart to forgive me and give me another chance."

Now he heard soft crying from her end. "Do you really mean it?"

"Yes. I'm so sorry I hurt you. I'm so sorry I ruined our beautiful relationship. If you'll give me another chance, I'll do my best never to hurt you again. I can't promise because I'm a flawed human being, but I will do my best."

"I will, too," she said, choking on a sob.

"You will? You'll give me another chance?" His heart danced with joy, each beat a promise for a wonderful future.

"Yes, Cam. I love you."

"Can I come see you this weekend?"

"I can't wait."

~

Cam didn't have to stand outside Olivia's door nervously fingering the ring box in his pocket this time because the minute he pulled up outside her apartment, she flung open the door and raced into his arms. He lifted her off the ground, spinning her in a delighted circle as she giggled. Then he set her down and claimed her lips with his. How good she tasted. It had been so long.

"Come inside. We don't want the neighbors to talk," she said, laughing, as she tugged on his hand.

"I don't care. Let them be jealous." But he allowed her to lead him inside, where she closed the door behind them and rose on tiptoe for another kiss.

"Uncle Cam!" cried Brian, racing into the room and throwing his chubby arms around Cam's waist. "Is it okay if I call you Uncle Cam?"

Cam looked from Olivia to Brian, then fell to one knee and reached for the ring box. He heard Olivia's strangled cry as he held the box between them.

"Well, to be honest," he said. "I was kind of hoping you might call me Daddy."

Chapter Thirty-Three
(One Year Later)

"Look at me, Daddy!" Brian trotted his pony around the riding arena, his face lit up in a big grin. The pony's hooves kicked up the dry dust into a cloud that swallowed his cousin who rode right behind him.

Finn yelled, "Look at me, Uncle Cam!" He coughed and backed off from following Brian so closely.

Olivia leaned on the fence watching the boys. She couldn't ever remember being happier. "Remember not to hold the reins so tightly, Brian," she called.

Cam pulled her to his side and rested his chin on the top of her head. "Those boys will make great cowboys one day."

"They don't have any choice," she replied. "They sure love it here."

"You do, too, right?" He looked down at his beautiful wife. *Wife*! He couldn't get over it. Who would have thought God would have blessed him with a perfect wife and ready-made family, not to mention his own ranch? Uncle John had officially turned over the title of the land to Cam, although he and Aunt Ruth still lived in the big ranch house and worked several days a week.

"You know I do. I can't imagine being anywhere else." Her eyes shone with love as she returned his gaze. "Except for one little problem."

His eyebrows drew together. "What problem?"

"Our bunk house is a bit small."

"Small? I thought you liked our little house. It's big enough for the three of us."

"I do. But it won't be big enough for the four of us."

He released her and stared at her, his eyes growing wide. "Are you saying—"

"We should be welcoming a new little cowboy or cowgirl next spring. Right around calving season."

Tears stung his eyes as he crushed her in a hug. "I can't believe it."

She wiggled out of his stifling embrace. "Why not? After working on a ranch all your life, you do know how these things happen, don't you?"

"You're amazing. I am the luckiest man on Earth."

She shot him a mischievous grin. "Well, I'm still not much of a cook."

"No argument there." They both laughed before he bent his head for a long kiss.

THANK YOU, DEAR READER

If you enjoyed reading this book, the best thing you can do to help the author is to tell others about it. Ellen would also greatly appreciate you rating her book and leaving a brief review at amazon.com and goodreads.com. Simply type in the name of the book and the author. When the website comes up, click on the picture of the book, scroll down, and there will be a button to click to leave a rating and a review. A review doesn't have to be long—a sentence or two telling what you liked about the book. Was it interesting, humorous, informative, thought-provoking, etc.? Thank you so much for your support.

Ellen would love for you to visit her website: https://ellenfannonauthor.com and subscribe to follow her weekly blog, *Good for a Laugh.*
Follow Ellen on Facebook: https://www.facebook.com/ellenfannonauthor

<u>SAVE THE DATE</u>
2022 Christian Indie Award Winner

What if you were given the chance to rekindle the flame with your first love? What happened to all those girls who were mean to you in school? Should Hannah Jensen take the chance of attending her high school reunion to find out?

Hannah hasn't been back to her hometown in twenty-five years. Now a widow raising a teenaged daughter, she has the opportunity to go home for her twenty-fifth high school reunion. The invitation to the reunion stirs up a lot of old memories at the same time she is dealing with loneliness, the challenges of single-parenting a teenager, people who want to "set her up" with eligible men, her own insecurities, and her eccentric family.

The story interweaves the present with scenes from Hannah's past and her fantasy of "happily ever after" with her high school boyfriend in a humorous and entertaining manner. Her feelings from being "shunned" by the cool kids resurface as she reflects back on her time as a teenager. There are several roadblocks on Hannah's journey from a teenager through her present. The growing pains and amusing situations in which she finds herself are ones to which we all can relate. As she walks the path of self-discovery, she also discovers the most important life lesson of all–her relationship to God.

<u>DON'T BITE THE DOCTOR</u>

Real doctors treat more than one species. At least that's what veterinarian, Jill Bennet tells herself. On

any given day, she may find herself doctoring dogs, cats, bunnies, birds, horses, pigs, or any other furry or feathered patient who crosses her path—striving daily to deliver compassion and competence to all God's creatures, in accordance with Colossians 3:23. Now, with over forty years of practice under her belt, Jill reflects back to her time as a new, young veterinarian in the early eighties—a time when women veterinarians were just beginning to become a presence among the previously male-dominated profession. Out in the real world, Jill finds herself in situations never covered in veterinary school. It is a journey of learning and laughter, as Jill contends with a variety of animal patients and their eclectic humans attached to the other end of the leash (and the checkbook), as well as less-than-helpful co-workers. Interwoven into this mix of new experiences is her budding romance with the owner of the sock-eating Labrador Retriever. *Don't Bite the Doctor* promises to bring smiles and tears to anyone who has ever been owned by an animal.

OTHER PEOPLE's CHILDREN

As a mid-thirties childless woman, Robin has all the answers on proper parenting. It doesn't take long, however, for Robin to realize that her perfect parenting ideas and reality often collide – the result being an amusing journey of finding out that God, indeed, has a sense of humor. As she deals with the baggage, idiosyncrasies, unique personalities, and special gifts of each child that crosses her path, she finds that there is no "one-size fits all" to parenting. However, in spite of the challenges she and her husband face, they are determined to become the children's strongest advocates in a flawed system that often fails the very victims it is designed to protect. The journey is often heartbreaking and frustrating, but these foster parents are firmly resolved that for whatever time they have children in their care, the children will know they are safe, protected, and loved by God, as well as by their foster parents.

HONOR THY FATHER EPISODE ONE

HONOR THY FATHER EPISODE TWO

Why should Adam's

daughters, with whom he hasn't had contact for twenty-five years, honor him now when he needs a life-saving bone marrow transplant? Why should his son, who was kicked out of the house, honor his father? Is there any hope of reconciliation when twenty-five years of anger, bitterness, and divergent pathways have led family members down different roads of life? *Honor Thy Father* is the compelling story of loss and redemption and how God can turn tragedy into triumph.

How does a family survive after being torn apart? Adam Wallace copes with the heartbreaking loss of his wife and daughters by immersing himself in his work. Charlotte withdraws from everyone and everything around her. Dana, living a life of privilege, does not even realize her loss. Katrina copes by trying to make everyone else happy. Scott copes by rebellion. Ultimately, they all come to realize that God can work through every situation to make beauty out of ashes.

LOVE IN THE WIND
Book 1 in the Love in the Wind Series

2024 Living Water Award Winner

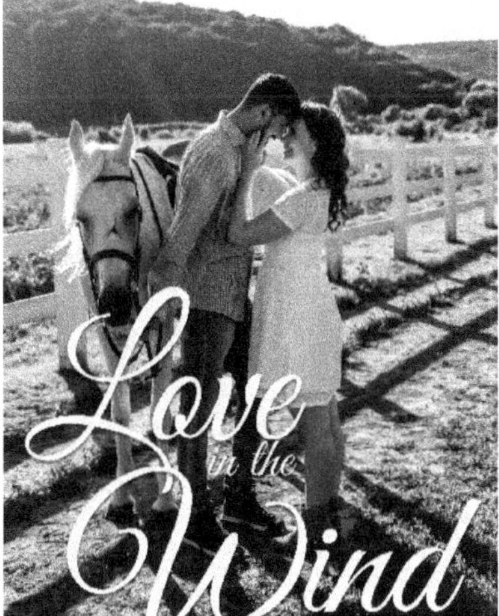

Wyoming rancher, Ben Parish, is struggling to keep his ranch afloat. Veterinarian, Darcy Fuller has moved to Wyoming to start a new life but is struggling to become established in a new area. Both have been badly burned by past relationships and are not looking to become involved in another. When their paths cross, Darcy has an idea to bring extra income to the ranch, as well as provide her with an outlet for her passion for working with horses. But can their growing attraction coexist with a business partnership?

FALLING FOR A COWBOY
Book 2 of the Love in the Wind Series

Biology professor, Kendra Clark, is an independent, competent, intelligent woman of faith—that is, until she is around cowboy, Ricky Gaither. Then she becomes a babbling klutz. For his part, Ricky doesn't have much use for intellectuals or God. But when they keep running into each other, they can't deny their growing attraction. Can a relationship work between two people who seem to have nothing in common? Or does the secret Ricky harbors make them more alike than Kendra realizes? And will that secret derail any hope for a relationship?